SEPTEMBER 2018

ED
  I HOPE YOU AND OWEN
ENJOY THIS ADVENTURE.

  MICHAEL CHANDLER

KINCADE'S BLOOD

⊶Michael Chandler⊷

PELICAN PUBLISHING COMPANY
GRETNA 2008

*The word "Pelican" and the depiction of a pelican are trademarks
of Pelican Publishing Company, Inc., and are registered in the
U.S. Patent and Trademark Office.*

Library of Congress Cataloging-in-Publication Data

Chandler, Michael.
  Kincade's blood / by Michael Chandler.
    p. cm.
  ISBN-13: 978-1-58980-530-9 (alk. paper) 1. Revenge—Fiction.
I. Title.
  PS3603.H35725K56 2008
  813'.6—dc22

                                        2008009903

Printed in the United States of America

Published by Pelican Publishing Company, Inc.
1000 Burmaster Street, Gretna, Louisiana 70053

On the high plains outside of Denver, Colorado, there lives a great-grandmother. Now in her eighties, she and her husband are the descendents of brave pioneers who migrated west in wagon trains.

Her ancestors eventually settled in Julesburg, opening Dye Hardware. His traveled to Northern California, but not before their wagon overturned crossing a flooded North Platte River, where the family lost their smallest baby Lena in the raging waters.

The great-grandmother's name is Loahna Chandler.

Loahna, thank you for your enthusiasm, your literary skills, your suggestions, and your many years of storytelling. It is to you that I humbly dedicate the story of *Kincade's Blood*.

KINCADE'S
BLOOD

1

The white-hot sun scorched the rimrock one last time before making its retreat below the western horizon. Off to the east a dust devil swirled up, whipping the mesquite, suddenly choking off the diminishing rays of the setting sun and filtering its remains into smoky shafts of light.

Something green and loathsome crawled onto a nearby boulder, its forked tongue smelling the air.

Kincade's eyes snapped open. Had he fallen asleep from exhaustion or passed out from pain? Either way, he must guard against it happening again.

He raised himself on one elbow. God, how that hurt! His deep blue eyes slowly scanned the horizon. No sign of riders. The sheriff's posse tracking him must have been fooled when he crossed the slick rock and doubled back into the arroyo. He collapsed back onto the sand and slowly closed his eyes again. He couldn't have been out long, for the coals of the campfire he had struggled to build had just reached the temperature for the job that had to be done.

The searing pain in his left shoulder triggered an involuntary grinding of teeth and clenching of fists. How bad was it? He tore open his bloodied shirt, which was caked with red soil, and stared at the wound. He had seen bullet holes that were smaller and bigger but none that appeared more fatal. Blood oozed from the torn flesh. Kincade knew if he didn't get that bullet out he would die.

What's it gonna be, Kincade? he thought to himself. You can't get Logan if your bones are bleaching in this desert. Get on with it.

Kincade whistled to his palomino, Gold Digger, who obediently trotted to his side. He grimaced as he pulled down the worn saddlebags and rummaged inside for the surgeon's tool. The instrument, once shiny but now blackened with use, measured a foot long. One end held two steel ovals, the first for a thumb, and the second for an index finger—much like a pair of seamstress scissors. At the other end of the shaft, two tiny claws faced each other, each half the size of one of the buttons on Kincade's shirt. The surgeon's tool was meant to probe, to root around, and to grab hold. He had used it on others, but this would be the first time he had tried it on himself.

Kincade jammed the device into the red-hot coals of the campfire. Whatever microscopic bugs made their home on that steel were now in the process of meeting their maker. As the coals crackled, the green reptile scurried across the boulder, disappearing into a deep crack. Within minutes, the steel glowed with the same heat and intensity as the fire itself.

Reaching out with his right hand, Kincade slowly withdrew the tool from the glowing embers, throwing a small shower of sparks. He opened the claws to the width of a .45-caliber Colt slug. With his left hand, Kincade jammed the rein of Gold Digger's bridle between his jaws, and bit down hard.

Damn Logan, thought Kincade. Damn him to hell. His hatred of his mortal enemy was now deeper, uglier, more vicious than the bullet that hid three inches beneath his skin where it had slammed into the bone. But this was not the

time for revenge. It would come; Kincade promised himself
. . . it would come.

Seconds after the twin claws disappeared into the jagged
wound, moments after Kincade's teeth bit deep into the latigo,
Gold Digger's nostrils flared wide at the smell of burning flesh.
The palomino's head instinctively jerked back. But not a
sound came from Kincade as the probe went deeper, seeking
Logan's bullet, its lead head now flared from target impact.

The claw hands bumped into the spent bullet, nudging it
deeper into the wound by a fraction of an inch, just enough
to send any man into convulsions. But not Kincade. The
hate-filled fire in his gut for what Wil Logan had done to
him far outstripped the unimaginable pain now coursing
through his left shoulder.

His fingers parted, the claws parted, the fingers closed,
the claws closed, and the disfigured bullet began to be
drawn out of the torn muscle. The palomino jerked again as
the smell became even stronger.

And then it was out.

Kincade spat the rein from his mouth, dropped the tool,
and with his right hand reached for and cracked open the
container of spoiled meat that had been in his saddlebags
one week too long. He jammed his fingers into a squirming
knot of freshly hatched white maggots, retrieving a palm-
sized colony, brought the nest across his chest, and spilled
the wriggling mass of larvae into the open bullet wound.
The grubs would clean the gash, just as the old Indian had
taught him so long ago.

The sun disappeared. The light shafts vaporized. The air
went still.

"You've slowed me, but you haven't stopped me. I'll get
you, Logan. If it's the last thing I do, I'll get you."

Kincade blacked out . . .

2

Jethro Wilcox could not have loved his little Melissa more if he had had her a hundred years instead of just six. And the miracle was that she loved him back. Only one other female had ever loved him: Melissa's mother. The two looked so much alike. Seeing his daughter around the cabin made him think that a little bit of Emily was still with him.

Jethro and Emily had come west to Nebraska when they were both nineteen—full of plans that only young people can dream. Melissa had been born before the year was out. Life was harder than they had expected, but they had each other and their daughter. She was now three, and Emily was expecting their second child. They hoped for a son. Then the horrifying afternoon changed everything forever.

Emily had spent most of that morning on the porch, churning butter. Melissa played in the yard with Dolly, pretending, laughing, and trying to be as good a mother as Emily was to her. Jethro stood at the edge of the clearing not far from Melissa, sweating profusely as he gave a stubborn tree stump another good whacking with his ax. Between strikes, Jethro could hear the soft scrape of the churn's wooden handle passing up and down, up and down, turning the milk inside. Their life was hard, but sweet—even sweeter than Emily's delicious butter.

When Jethro looked to the east and saw the dust rising from five fast-approaching horses, he knew trouble was imminent. "Emily! Get inside and bolt the door!" He dropped the ax and rushed over to Melissa, grabbing her up in his arms.

"What's the matter, Papa? You're squeezing Dolly and me."

"I have to hide you in the root cellar, Melissa." He was running as fast as he could.

"I don't like the root cellar, Papa."

"I know, but it's safe." She began to cry. "Dolly will keep you company." He placed her inside and gave her a kiss. "Hush, my darling," he whispered. "Be very quiet, and Papa will come for you as soon as he can. I promise."

He shut the cellar door and ran to get his rifle, which hung above the mantel. He took a circuitous route back to the cabin through the cornfield so the cellar wouldn't be spotted. When he emerged from the tall stalks, he shouted to Emily, "Let me in!" But when she lifted the heavy bolt, two of the strange men slid from their horses like lightning, kicked open the door, and shoved Emily outside.

Two others grabbed Jethro before he could reach the house. He cursed and struggled, but they were too strong for him. They tied him to the chopping block in the yard, chest down, arms behind, head yanked savagely up by the hair so Jethro was forced to face his terrified wife. The two who had Emily pushed her to her knees. Powerful hands held her fast as she screamed to Jethro for help.

In the midst of the dust, the terror, and the commotion, one thing remained as still as a stone. The biggest, ugliest of the five was still on his horse, motionless as a statue, his dead black eyes riveted on Emily. Not a twitch came from the enormous brute as he waited for his four men to finish their preparation of the hellish nightmare to come.

The yard fell silent. The four men looked up to the fifth, their leader. They had seen him with that look before. No words were exchanged. They backed off. It was obvious that the butcher's table had been set. Emily tried to scream, but the terror was frozen in her throat.

The outlaw slowly removed his gloves, one finger at a time. The saddle leather creaked as he shifted his considerable weight into the left stirrup. Drawing his right leg up, over, and then down, this dark figure lowered his heavy body to the ground, never once taking his eyes off Emily. Jethro squirmed with all his might, struggling to break free of the four hands and bonds pinning him to the chopping block. But he was held in a vice.

"Leave her alone!" Jethro shouted as one of the two men holding his head removed a filthy rag from around his throat, stuffing it in Jethro's mouth so deeply that it made Emily's husband gag. "Shussh," hissed the bandit in a whisper so soft that Jethro's terror increased tenfold. "Shussh . . ."

The leader walked slowly toward Emily. The only sound in the yard was that of the relentless Nebraska wind, and the footfall of the fifth bandit's boots in the dirt. His empty right hand snaked out, and then slithered back under the filthy frock coat he wore, past his waist, and into the small of his back. There was a chilling pause, and then the hand slowly returned. But now it clutched an enormous knife, one like Jethro had never seen, the blade at least eight inches long and three inches wide. By the flash of the sun, all could see that this knife held the sharpness of a barber's razor.

The man stood in front of the kneeling Emily, the knife at his right leg, the blade imperceptibly moving back and forth as if it were a caged animal about to be set free. Blessedly, Emily passed out.

The steel began to rise toward the woman's face. Never in Jethro's entire life had he felt such terror. He reflexively clenched his eyes shut. One of the two men holding him fast kneeled down at Jethro's side, producing another smaller but equally sharp knife. Holding it less than an inch from the young man's eyes, he whispered in Jethro's ear.

"Close 'em one more time, and I'll remove both your eyelids. Shussh . . ." and the man stood, looking to the leader as though to say, "Go ahead."

In all his days, in all the days that would follow, Jethro Wilcox had never, would never again, witness anything so cruel and grotesque as what happened to his sweet and innocent Emily at the hands of this monster.

Never.

As hardened and evil as the four outlaws were, even they swallowed as their leader worked the blade. They knew better than to say anything or to move even the lightest muscle. In what seemed like an eternity, even for this bunch of lowlife trash, the fiendish brute finished, wiped the blade on his boot, stood, and returned the weapon to the sheath at the small of his back. Not once had he uttered one word. Jethro sobbed and moaned with indescribable torment.

"What about him, Wil?" one asked, pointing at the bound Jethro.

"Let him join her in heaven," the leader mocked, crossing himself with a hairy hand. So they pistol-whipped him and left him for dead. The five outlaws took everything from the cabin worth having, and before riding away, set the rest on fire.

Jethro Wilcox would have died willingly but for the little girl waiting for him in the root cellar. He kept breathing for her sake. His body and hands had lost all feeling. Everything was black before him. He heard the cracking flames and fall of timbers as the cabin burned.

Then he heard the rumble of wagon wheels and a familiar

voice. "Jethro! Jethro! I saw the smoke from my field. My God, what's happened here?" It was his nearest neighbor, Howard Phillips, who lived five miles down the road. He jumped from the buckboard and ran to him. He knelt at Jethro's side, removing the knotted ropes that bound Jethro to the chopping block.

"Oh, my God. Look what they did to Emily."

"Can you cover her with something, Howard?"

He walked back to the buckboard, removing a blanket from the box, returned to what was left of Emily, and enclosed the body.

"Help me up. Melissa's in the root cellar. I've got to go to her."

With great effort, Jethro staggered toward his daughter. "I'm coming, my darling, I'm coming," he kept calling.

When he pushed open the doors she ran to him. "Papa! Oh Papa! Please don't ever leave me alone again." He lifted her in his trembling arms and kissed her wet cheeks again and again. "I won't ever. I promise you."

When they returned to the yard, Howard had raked over the blood in the dusty yard and lifted Emily's covered body into the bed of the buckboard, making sure Melissa had no idea what lay beneath the thick blanket. He helped them both onto the seat and flicked the reins to set the mule going. "Stay with us, Jethro. You stay with us . . ."

Jethro sat on the buckboard, clutching Melissa, not hearing a word Howard said. Just once he looked back as they headed down the rutted road. Small flames still licked the cabin he and Emily had loved so much. The only thing left standing was the stone chimney.

In the days and weeks that followed, Jethro gained back his strength. The two men made a coffin for Emily, burying her next to Howard's first wife and three young children on the hilltop. Howard never urged him to leave nor questioned him about his future plans.

One Sunday after church Melissa softly asked her father the question she had kept inside her for weeks. "Did Mama go to heaven?"

Jethro smiled his sad, lonely smile. "I'm sure she did." And he thought, She's already been in hell.

Melissa clung to the memory of her mother in sweet, childish ways. She would sit for hours with Dolly at the windswept grave, making chains of wildflowers or telling the wooden cross what had happened during her day. Her vigil seemed to make her happy rather than sad.

Jethro only returned to the burned-out homestead once. There was a metal strongbox buried beneath the hearthstones, which he felt the outlaws had not found nor the fire destroyed. It contained the deed to the homestead and a little money they had saved. He looked around and wept. He had no heart to rebuild—too many memories, both sweet and sad.

That night he told Howard, "Guess it's time for me and Melissa to move on—to start over, my friend. I'd be much obliged if you'd sell me your buckboard and mule."

"Tell you what. You deed over your homestead to me, and you can have both. Okay?"

"Okay. Thanks for your friendship and . . ." Jethro's words trailed off.

"I understand. If you ever want to come back, it's all yours again."

Jethro and Melissa headed west to the plains of Colorado.

Julesburg was a thriving settlement near the South Platte River. He built a one-room cabin about a half-hour's ride away, not far from the well-worn wagon train ruts of the never ending, forever moving Oregon Trail.

3

In the next several years it had been Melissa who had turned Jethro from a grieving shadow of a man to a father with unbridled love and compassion. She was more than the apple of his eye—she was his reason for living. Instead of being bitter he became tenderhearted, not only toward her, but toward all persons who showed admiration for his daughter. And why wouldn't they? She was precious in her looks and her behavior. Her freckles . . . the way she would toss her blond curls aside with an upward "poosh" of air, her generous and oftentimes chapped lips, her way of telling everyone, "I'm going on seven, you know." But her most incredible and transforming power were four little words given only to him: "I love you, Papa." Melissa had returned sanity and then joy to Jethro's life.

Jethro knew he needed to find a mother for Melissa. There were things a woman needed to teach a little girl—to explain to her as she grew older. But he didn't look too hard because his memories of Emily were still so strong. When he and Melissa took the buckboard into Julesburg the school-marm and the seamstress flirted outrageously with him, making a fuss over his little girl, hoping that this handsome, eligible man would notice how maternal they were. He would glance down at Melissa who would be smiling and telling them, "I'm going on seven, you know." She looked so much like her mother that Jethro would find an excuse to leave and get on with their errands.

There was one widow, however, for whom he had feelings, however brief. She had ridden up to their cabin one evening. She was kind of pretty, but her eyes were red and puffy, probably from crying. She slipped from her horse and came toward Jethro who put down the hoe he was using. She was about Emily's height, her head almost reaching his shoulder. But she was as gaunt as a rail whereas Emily had been a bit plump.

"Excuse me . . . Hello, I'm Cissy Dye. My husband and I have been travelin' with the wagon train. Our family had a bushel of terrible luck." Her eyes became wet, and her lower lip trembled.

"Howdy, I'm Jethro Wilcox. Why don't you tell me about it, Mrs. Dye? Maybe I can help." He took her arm and led her to the porch.

Cissy settled into one of the rockers and nervously twisted a small rag of a handkerchief in her fingers. "We started with six wagons in our train. We were travelin' on the south side of the river, but we had to cross to the north side to continue on the trail to Wyoming. You know the place where most folks cross?"

"I surely do. Someday they'll have to put a ferry or a bridge there."

She smiled weakly. "Maybe, but it ain't gonna help me. You seen the water at that crossing right now?"

"No, but the whole river has been at flood stage for almost a month."

"I know. When we come there, the wagon master said the

high water would go down if we waited. But it didn't go down and didn't go down. We waited six days, but it was still ragin'. The wagon master said it was too dangerous to put our wagons in that water, but some of the men began to worry about the Sierra Nevada Mountains up ahead getting covered with snow before we could cross them. They persuaded the wagon master to go ahead." Her handkerchief was knotted, and her voice was shaky.

"Our wagon master wrote six numbers on papers and put them in his hat. Each man drew one out to decide in what order the wagons would cross. Mr. Dye drew the number six, so we was to go last.

"The first wagon was pulled by two big farm horses. They barreled into the river which was all rollin' and frothy. We all watched, scared to death. But the horses were very strong, and they made it to shore about a quarter mile downstream. We all cheered."

"That wagon was lucky. Did the rest of you follow?"

"Oh yes. The men were all encouraged and excited to try. They pulled their wagons into a line along the bank ready to go."

"Mr. Dye too?"

"Well, kind of." She turned her head away and dabbed at her eyes. "My husband was the oldest, you see, and didn't have the courage of the young bucks. While we waited he kept pacin' back and forth, and I heard him mutterin', 'I can't swim. I can't swim.' But pretty soon it was gonna be our turn. We'd let our boys run around while we waited, but now we had to load everyone in the wagon. It was real crowded 'cause usually most of us walked alongside."

"How many are in your family, Mrs. Dye?"

"Well, there was Mr. Dye, of course. And we had six young-uns. And we had to bring Miz Sadie, Mr. Dye's mother, 'cause she's got a brother in California that we's goin' to ranch with." Her eyes dropped to her lap. "She don't like me much."

Jethro chuckled. "I can't understand why." She smiled a little. Then, swallowing hard, she continued.

"Miz Sadie was holdin' my little girl Lena on one side of the wagon. I had the three littlest boys with me across from her. Our two biggest ones was with Mr. Dye up front 'cause they was all shoutin' at our two oxen to get 'em goin'. We thought things was goin' pretty well even though some water was comin' in the floorboards. Then all of a sudden, comin' from nowhere, big logs started poundin' on us." Her voice was rising with fright.

"Miz Sadie said some cabin must have been washed away upstream. The wagon rocked and rocked, and the oxen got scared and pulled us this way and that. One big log tore off the wagon canvas. Another busted into the side." She was almost screaming as she relived the terror.

"We was all yellin' to Mr. Dye to do somethin', but he was more scared than any of us. All of a sudden the whole wagon turned over, and we was all throwed in the water. Everything we owned was carried downstream in a big rush. I couldn't see nobody else. I was swirlin' and dippin' and gulpin' water. I knew I was drownin'. Then all of a sudden one of the strong young men from the wagon train had me under my arms. He had a rope tied around his waist, and he signaled somebody on the bank to pull on the rope so's we'd come up outta the water. And that's how I come to be alive, Mr. Wilcox."

"And what about the others?"

"Well, the five boys and Miz Sadie had been pulled out too. Nobody had rescued Mr. Dye 'cause he was a big, heavy man. I guess they wanted to help us women and children

first. They found him after about an hour. His head had hit
a big rock and busted open. They buried him without me
lookin'."

Jethro did not detect any sadness when Cissy talked about
her husband. "You said you had six children, Mrs. Dye?"

"Yes I did. But I don't now." She began to sob and could-
n't say anything for several minutes. Then she added softly,
"Nobody pulled little Lena outta the water."

Jethro didn't know what to say to comfort her. "I'm so
sorry. I really am."

"No, you couldn't understand—nobody can understand.
She was my life—my reason for livin'."

Jethro Wilcox flashed back to the Nebraska horror. He
paused, then said, "But I do understand, Mrs. Dye. Much
more than you know."

"Ya do?" She breathed a heavy sigh and stared at him with
dark, forlorn eyes.

He wanted to help her so much. "How old are you, Mrs.
Dye?"

She looked down at her lap. "I know I don't look it, but
I'm just nineteen."

Jethro remembered that was Emily's age when they came
west. "And you've had six children?"

"Seven, actually—one a year since I was thirteen. The last
one died. But he was just another boy anyhow."

Would he and Emily have had so many children by now if
she had lived?

"My pa sold me to Mr. Dye when I was twelve 'cause he
needed the money, and they was friends. Mr. Dye was an old
man—maybe forty or more. But he treated me okay, I guess.
He was sure proud of all the boys I birthed for him."

Once again her eyes filled with tears, and her lower lip
trembled. "And then I had Lena—a little girl. And she was

mine—all mine. I finally had a little daughter and a reason for livin'. Mr. Dye hardly looked at her, but she was my angel—my gift from God. Now she's gone, and I don't want to live no more. But Miz Sadie says I gotta because of the boys." She burst into heartrending sobs. "Can you understand that, Mr. Wilcox?"

He understood it all too well. Without thinking he pulled her into his arms and gently rocked her back and forth. "I do understand, Mrs. Dye. That's the way I feel about my Melissa. I couldn't bear it if anything happened to her."

They stayed embraced for maybe a minute. Suddenly Cissy Dye felt herself feeling better, maybe even good. It struck Jethro, for just a moment, that this young woman—so soft and dependent—reminded him of his Emily. Then Cissy Dye pulled away, wiped her face, and stood up.

"The men folks have looked and looked for Lena. Now they say the train has to get goin' again."

"Will you go along?" he asked.

"Oh yes. Miz Sadie is arrangin' everythin' with the other folks." She took his big hand in one of her small ones. "I come here to ask a favor of you since you live so close to the river." She reached in her pocket and pulled out a little tin box, holding it toward Jethro. "My mama give this to me. It once held tea from China." Tears slowly fell from her innocent eyes. "Mr. Wilcox, if you find the body of my little Lena, would you please cut me one of her brown curls and a little piece of the dress she was wearin'—blue calico—and send it to me? The wagon master says to mail it to the U.S. Government Sacramento Fort, California. Could you do that please?"

"I'd be more than happy to."

"You see, when I die I want that curl and calico to be placed over my heart." She gave him a quick kiss on the cheek. "You're a very kind man, Mr. Wilcox. Good-bye." She ran to her grazing horse, mounted quickly, and rode away to the promise of California. But Cissy Dye, and what remained of her family, would never make it.

Melissa had been watching and listening from around the corner of the cabin. She ran to Jethro and hugged his legs. "Papa, you must always hold my hand tight when we cross the river, even if we're in the buckboard."

Jethro picked up his daughter and held her close. "We'll never cross the river if there's any danger. I promise." Nothing bad must ever happen to his precious child.

Six weeks later Jethro found the swollen body of little Lena wedged between rocks in a tangle of river willow. He carefully snipped the lock of hair and cut a tiny square of the calico from what was left of her dress. He wondered about putting a note in the box too, asking how Mrs. Dye was getting along. Then he thought better of it. No use starting something neither of them would be able to finish. He had time yet to let Melissa grow up without a woman's hand. Of course it wouldn't hurt to put his return address on the package. He buried the little white body by himself without Melissa seeing. He placed stones in the shape of a cross to mark the grave of Cissy Dye's angel.

It was another three weeks before Jethro and Melissa took the buckboard into Julesburg to mail the box to California. The day was warm but not hot, and the prairie flowers were blooming everywhere. He watched her bobbing head and listened to her happy chatter. She had on a yellow calico smock and a red sunbonnet with her hair escaping underneath. I must cut off a lock of those golden curls and get a snip of that calico, he thought. Should anything happen to me I'd ask to have them placed over my heart to remember this perfect day. He would remember it all right—but not for happy reasons.

For the horror of what happened to the Dye family that spring at the South Platte River was nothing compared to what was in store for little Melissa and her adoring father, fourteen days after Kincade had ripped a .45-caliber slug from his left shoulder.

As Jethro and Melissa were entering Julesburg, five vicious men approached the outskirts of town. They were led by a burly, bearded, filthy piece of trash named Wil Logan.

4

Kincade had his old nightmare again.

The boys had scuffled, and one's shirt had been torn open. Kincade backed away.

"Whatcha got there?" the other boy yelled. "What's that little leather bag with all them shiny Injun beads? Lemme see."

"No way. Not showin' ya nothin'. It's mine."

"I'll make you sorry if you don't lemme see it."

"Can't show ya 'cause it's got my secret."

"Then, Kincade, I'm gonna kill you for it." A young Wil Logan pulled a Bowie knife from the back of his belt. "Bet you never knowed I had this." Wil whipped the wickedly sharp blade in a vicious roundhouse over his head. "You got your secret—I got mine." He laughed, and saliva dripped down his chin.

Logan began stalking forward, swinging the steel back and forth. Kincade ducked and dodged as the knife flashed and sliced the air. Then it scraped Kincade's throat, slicing a good four inches of flesh, throwing fountains of blood in a splashing arch.

Kincade jerked up, instinctively raising his right hand to

block the next blow. He opened his eyes, and looked into the snout of his tawny palomino, Gold Digger.

Kincade shook his head to clear it. Raising himself up on one elbow, he patted the velvety nose that poked him. "How long was I out, Digger?"

"Chuff," the horse snorted.

"That long, huh?" He lay down again and stared at the immense sky. Would the dream ever leave him? Would Wil Logan ever fade out of his life?

He wished he had the old Indian's dream catcher. Just a small hoop with a web of sweet grass strung side to side. Beautiful feathers of small birds hung from the edge. In the center was a tiny blue turquoise nugget. The old Indian had told him to place the dream catcher near his head at night. Dreams both good and bad would fall from the sky into the web of the hoop. The Indian knew the blue stone sentinel let the good dreams pass into the sleeping boy's mind. The bad dreams were held back by the turquoise, trapped in the sweet grass until daylight returned, its warmth evaporating their evil, banishing them to the sky overhead.

The dream catcher had worked so well for Kincade when he was a boy. He wondered if it could work now to drive out the nightmare he suffered as an adult.

Wil Logan had always hated Kincade. From the day the old Indian had first brought Kincade into town, the chemistry was explosive.

Kincade couldn't remember how long he had been with the old Indian. His earliest memory was yelling his own name—"It's Kincade! Kincade!"—whenever the old Indian tried to call him something else.

He had little evidence of his life before he met the old Indian. His only clue was the color of his skin, the fading memory of a white woman, and a strange symbol carved into his right bicep. This mark consisted of three lines, side by side. The middle of the three lines bowed slightly into a half moon, touching the first line about halfway down near the middle. The scar symbol stretched as he grew. As deep as it was, it would be with him the rest of his life.

It was Kincade's brand, almost like the ones he saw on cattle. Kincade was too busy to wonder about his past. Even when he was a very small boy the old Indian filled the days with teaching him the ways of the wild. Kincade learned how to gather and grow whatever could be eaten, woven, or stored for lean times. Then he was taught to kill animals for food. He became proficient with bow and arrow, rifle and knife, and even a sharp stone. He could tan a hide, and make britches, shirt, or moccasins. He could build a shelter and destroy all signs of a camp when they left. Kincade learned how to heal wounds and treat sicknesses using the natural medicines from the land, and from the creatures that crawled upon it.

The old Indian taught young Kincade through his watching, doing, by hand gestures and signs. The two had their own language . . . mostly Indian with a smattering of the white man's words. Only once did Kincade ask the old Indian why he lived alone and not with a tribe. There was silence for a long time. "I steal something that I want very bad from powerful brave. I not go back unless I return it. I not ready." And that was all he would say. Kincade thought, He's probably lost it by now and is too proud to admit it.

One day the old Indian told Kincade to mount his horse and follow. They rode farther than they had ever gone before, and for the first time the boy saw a white man's settlement. He had no idea why they had come there after all the years of living by themselves. The old Indian dismounted and motioned for Kincade to stay on his horse. He went to a porch and began talking in sign language to some white men.

Kincade sat on his horse and waited. It was a hot day, and he pulled off his buckskin shirt, folding it in front of him. A boy about his own age had been walking around and around the horse, staring at Kincade.

"Hey, you up there," the circling boy finally shouted. "What's your name?" Kincade didn't answer. "I said what's your name . . . your *name?* What's the matter, don't you speak English?"

"Kincade."

"That's a pretty dumb name. Kincade. Never heard such a dumb name before." He began throwing small rocks at the horse's rump, and the animal became skittish.

"You know that old redskin is trying to sell you? The highest bid so far is one rusty rifle and a jug of bad whiskey."

Kincade wondered to himself. What's this boy talking about? But again he said nothing until the old Indian came back with a rifle and a jug.

"What's happening?" Kincade asked him.

The old Indian put the jug in a bag slung around the neck of his horse, and he raised up the rifle. "These not for me. They for powerful brave of my tribe. I not give you back to him, but I bring him presents—good horse, good gun, good whiskey. He think it good trade, and he let me stay." He slung the rifle strap across his shoulder. "Put on shirt. Get off horse." Kincade did what he was told, still not believing what was happening.

The old Indian took a medicine bag from around his own neck and handed it to Kincade. The outside of the small pouch had pretty beads of various colors formed into the shape of a circle. "Put around neck," he whispered in their own language. "Keep inside shirt. Show no one. Has my secret on outside—your secret on inside."

The old Indian took the reins of Kincade's horse and climbed on his own. "You live here now. I go back to my tribe. You go back to yours. I die soon."

Kincade could sense great pain in the old Indian's eyes, but it wasn't from his aging flesh, but from something deep within his heart. No further words were shared. The old Indian . . . the only person Kincade had ever really known . . . left the boy standing in the dusty street with the bully laughing and pointing at him.

Kincade hurried to an alley. When he was sure he was totally alone and free from prying eyes, Kincade looked more carefully at the medicine bag. On the outside there were several circles. The largest circles had alternating dark blue and turquoise colored beads. The beads of the inner circle were rust and bright red.

Kincade carefully pulled the thongs to open the bag. He took out a scrap of carefully folded leather that had come from the same hide. His eyes grew wide with curiosity. The leather patch was about the size of his palm. There were blue, turquoise, rust, and red beads sewn on both sides. Looking at one side, Kincade was shocked to see that the bead design matched the symbol carved into his right bicep. Flipping the leather over, he saw that the second symbol was nearly the same. Not quite, but almost. The second symbol had five lines, not three like Kincade's. The first four of the five lines touched one another, and resembled a wicked bolt of lightning. The fifth and last line stood by itself, exactly matching Kincade's own final line.

Kincade was looking at the five lines, fingering the beads, when suddenly the scar on his right bicep began to ache, as though it had been torn open. Kincade reached up with his left hand, rubbing his scar. When he withdrew his hand, he almost expected to see blood on his fingers. But there was none. Just the ache.

The boy shrugged his shoulders, returned the beaded leather patch with its back-to-back symbols to the old Indian's medicine bag, tightened the drawstring, and then placed the narrow leather strap over this head and down onto his neck. Kincade tucked the bag safely over his heart.

Nobody wanted to take in the wild youngster named Kincade. But no one had the heart to send him packing. Slowly, very slowly, he learned to communicate in the white man's language, which sounded so foreign to his ears. He moved from person to person, from job to job. Sometimes he slept in a barn, sometimes in a store, often on the ground. He learned soon enough that he had to be good at whatever he was asked to do or he would never be asked again. He had to be dependable and honest, or word would get around, and no one would hire him. Kincade learned it was smart to be polite and courteous, especially to the women.

Every person, every job taught him something he filed away in his memory for future use. Folks were kind, especially when he was a kid. The blacksmith, whose bellows he pumped, taught him about forging iron. The owner of the general store taught him to drive a team and to deliver bulky goods to neighboring ranches scattered for miles around. At the livery stable he cared for the horses just as the old Indian had taught him, and he did it so well that the owner said he could live in the shed at the back. When it got cold he could come inside with the horses.

The schoolmarm said she would teach him to read if he would do chores and run errands for her. One day, as he was nearly halfway through the alphabet, the teacher pointed to the letter following "J."

"That's a 'K,'" she said. "Can you repeat that for me?" Suddenly, it struck him. "I know this one, ma'am. It's written on my arm." He pulled up his right sleeve and showed her. Initially grimacing at the thought of how the boy must have suffered when the brand had been carved into his arm, the schoolmarm recovered, saying, "That's right. The first line with the second line bowed into it forms a 'K.' Is that for your first name? 'K' for Kincade?"

The boy thought about that.

Then, she said, "What's the third line stand for? Is that for your last name?"

The scar on Kincade's right bicep began to ache. The boy realized, for the first time, that the three lines carved into his arm, and the three lines on the leather patch hidden within the old Indian's medicine bag, weren't lines at all. They were letters. And the first initial was his—"K." But there was no clue as to what the final vertical gash meant.

The discovery almost made the boy feel dizzy, and he briefly swayed. "Kincade," said the schoolmarm, wrinkling her brow in concern, "Are you all right?"

5

As Kincade grew older, he developed a habit that served him well. Having no personal possessions except the old Indian's beaded medicine bag, he would pick up and stow away any object that he thought might one day prove useful. His well-known collection of odds and ends amused most townsfolk, but it was his security cache. He collected big things like discarded carpenter tools and medical paraphernalia, and little things like scissors and brushes, stuffing them into the shed behind the livery. Since he had nothing, everything seemed important. The townsfolk didn't throw away anything without first asking, "Hey, Kincade, you want this?" He usually did. "Thank you. I do."

Kincade had only one enemy—Wil Logan. In the beginning, the bully made fun of the way this new kid talked, because often Kincade couldn't remember the English words for what he wanted to say. This heckling often turned into pushing, shoving, and tripping.

As Kincade matured, his boyish looks gave way to the beginnings of a rugged handsomeness. Girls were drawn to him. They would giggle and try to attract Kincade's attention by asking how it was to live with an Indian. These innocent flirtations sent Wil into jealous rage. When the girls left all in a twitter, he would throw stones or spoiled fruit at Kincade.

Kincade tried to stay away from Logan, but the boy would hunt him down, forcing Kincade to face up to his enemy and defend himself. They brawled with one another frequently. But Wil was always the victor, as his skills at fighting dirty were honed by trickery and deceit.

Kincade made one good friend, a boy about two years younger named Jesse Keller. Jesse's pa was a drunk. Jesse never saw him, and didn't want to. His ma had run off with a harness maker, and the way Jesse's pa had treated her, it was no wonder. The boy took shelter with a widow named Agnes Johnson. Her shack was so small that he had no space for himself. Agnes was always so busy trying to work at any job that would keep body and soul together that she had little time for Jesse. She was nothing like family. Jesse had to look out for himself, just like Kincade.

Sometimes, the two found jobs together. They became real pards. Kincade taught Jesse how to swim and climb trees, to catch fish in the river and frogs in the swamp. Jesse taught Kincade how to talk better, to laugh and joke. As the schoolteacher taught Kincade to read, Kincade passed along all he learned to Jesse. When their voices were changing they even took a crack at singing together, but got to laughing so hard at their screeches and howls that they decided to give that up quick.

They talked about girls, and the mystery under all the ruffles and lace. Kincade even showed Jesse the symbol "K" on his arm and the old Indian's medicine bag. "Wow. Wish I had somethin' like that," the younger boy said.

One evening Kincade and Jesse were stretched out on their backs in a field of wild prairie grass. The sun was setting, and the sky was particularly pretty. They hadn't said much, just looked. Then Kincade rolled over to face his friend. "Jess, why do you think Wil hates me so much?"

"'Cause he's mean, through and through. Ain't got a good bone in his body."

"Why don't his ma and pa teach him better?"

"His ma's dead. Miz Agnes Johnson says she died of a broken heart."

"What's that mean?"

"I don't know. I asked Miz Agnes Johnson, and she got all fluttery and funny like. She said somethin' terrible happened. Then she wouldn't talk about it no more."

"What about his pa?"

"His pa's in the army and gone most all of the time. He brags that he was named for one of his pa's cavalry officers—Wilson. But his ma hated him and didn't want to call him her son, so she called him Wil."

"Who's he live with?"

"Some folks say he's got kin in town that won't have nothin' to do with him, so he stays with an old army friend of his pa. But he don't like Wil. Nobody does. You know that big rock that went through the window at the general store? Wil threw it. I seen him. And the tack that got stolen from the livery stable? He done that too."

"How come he don't pick on you?"

"Oh, he's mean to me too, when he remembers you and me is friends. Didn't I tell you about the frog?" Jesse asked.

"What frog?"

"Well, I was all by myself trying to catch frogs in the swamp, like you learned me. I finally got one and was holdin' it close to my chest. It was kinda funny, shakin' its head side to side 'n all. Wil Logan come up sudden behind me and yelled, 'Gimme that frog!' I said, 'Get your own, Wil. This one's for Kincade, 'cause he learned me how to catch 'em.'"

"That made Wil mad?" Kincade interrupted.

"Didn't seem like it right off. He said, 'I'll give it right back. Come on. I ain't never held a frog before.' I said, 'You promise?' And he nodded his head. 'Give it to me!' Then he snatched it away from me."

"And then?" asked Kincade.

"The little frog squirmed, legs springin' out and back again like he was tryin' to make a break for it. Wil took one of the back legs in each hand like they was in a vice, and, Kincade, he tore that little frog in half! He yelled, 'That's what'll happen to any friends 'a Kincade! I'll tear 'em apart!' Then he threw the two halves at me."

"Oh Jess. That's awful."

"I screamed and lunged at him. But I'm too little and skinny. He hit me good."

"Why didn't you tell me before? I woulda smashed him."

"You got enough trouble with Logan without me addin' any more."

"Jess, that's what friends are for—to stick together. Besides, he hasn't hurt me much yet. Just some bloody noses and black eyes. I can put up with that."

"I'd beat 'im up for you if I could, Kincade. But I'm too little and skinny." They both laughed. Jesse added, "Maybe when I grow some, we can stick together then."

When Jesse became a teenager, they celebrated by smoking two cigars and killing a bottle of whiskey behind the livery shed. "We're just like brothers," Jesse slurred. Kincade drained the last of the bottle. "Only better." They nodded to one another in full agreement, before falling into a stuporous sleep.

On Jesse's fourteenth birthday, Kincade took him to his first brothel. "Okay, Jess. Here's your dollar. Go at it."

"Ain't you comin' in too?"

"That's all the money I got. I'll wait for you right here."

Jesse reappeared in all of five or six minutes, shirttail askew. The two stepped off the boardwalk and into the street as Jesse licked his hand and tried to smooth down a persistent cowlick. "So, how was it for you, Jess?"

Jesse looked this way and that, and lowered his voice. "I gotta tell you, Kincade, not as good as I expected. Maybe if I practiced more . . ."

Kincade burst out laughing and put his arm around his friend. "Maybe. But from now on it's your dollar—not mine." And they swaggered down the street together.

When Kincade was seventeen, Jesse saved his life.

Wil Logan had become more and more brutal. His face would contort with hatred, and his swearing frighteningly obscene. He would charge and strike Kincade unmercifully until someone pulled him off. Kincade asked the blacksmith to teach him some punches, but even then he was no match for Wil's savagery. Twice Kincade was knocked out completely and Jesse brought him around with water before helping him back to his shed.

The day came when Wil stole a Bowie knife. He was just itching to use it, and knew who to use it on.

That fight had given Kincade nightmares ever after, because it was the first time that Logan had used a lethal weapon against him. He was surprised and shocked that Wil's hatred would go so far. Not like him? Yes. But slash his throat and nearly kill him? Kincade would have died there on the street if Jesse hadn't carried him to the doctor's office.

"You didn't get here any too soon," the doctor said as he quickly went to work. The younger boy stood and watched, visibly shaken with fear and anger at what Logan had done to his friend. When the job was done, Jesse said, "Will you do me a favor, Doc?"

"Sure, boy. You've earned it."

"Take your little knife there and cut me a design on my right arm just like he's got." Jesse rolled up Kincade's sleeve and pointed to the "K" next to a line on his bicep.

"That'll hurt. You sure you want me to do that?"

"More than anything." So the boy gritted his teeth while the doctor used his scalpel. Then Jesse took a fingertip of Kincade's still wet blood and rubbed it into the incision, mixing it with his own.

"Now we's not just brothers, we's blood brothers, ain't we?"

Kincade silently smiled and thought to himself, Forever and ever.

It was all so long ago. The miles Kincade had ridden over the years were supposed to have covered over those memories, at least the ugly ones. But Logan's bullet and the double-cross outside of Helena brought it all back, making the childhood hatred seem like yesterday.

Kincade sat up, shaking the cobwebs from his head as he squinted into the Montana sunrise. He stretched his injured left shoulder forward, up, back to the shoulder blade, down and back again. The bullet wound hurt like hell, but the blood had congealed as the maggots did their cleaning. Digger watched with indifference.

The fire had long since gone dead. Kincade looked toward his feet, and there in the dust lay the surgeon's tool, Logan's .45-caliber bullet held fast in the claws' grip. He picked it up, looking at the flared lead, flecked with his bone.

Suddenly, he felt the Bowie knife slicing his throat, Logan's eyes enraged, saliva running down Wil's chin as he relished the gore.

The nightmare.

Kincade gritted his teeth, but for only a split second. He picked up the saddlebags, opened a leather flap, and put the tool with Logan's spent bullet into the pouch. He walked up to Gold Digger, gently stroked his neck, and whispered, "Thanks for hangin' around, fella."

The palomino's large brown eyes were quiet as Kincade stretched to his full height. He was tall . . . about six feet six inches. He grabbed the stock of his lever-action Winchester 73 and jammed it securely into the saddle's scabbard. He handled the rifle like he had been born with it.

He pulled down the wide-brimmed buckaroo-crease hat he favored. The brim shaded his rugged face. Kincade wore a full-wrap wildrag around his throat, knotted close to the scar from Logan's Bowie so long ago.

Around his hips, Kincade wore a gunfighter's tie-down twin rig, one slung over the other, fifty cartridges per belt. Two pearl-handled Colts gleamed in well-worn holsters. If one were to look closely, he would see that each six-shooter's hammer serrations were worn nearly smooth by thumbs that could cock faster than chain lightning with a link snapped.

Leather braces over both shoulders were attached to trousers that fit his slender hips like a glove. Over his bib-front shirt, Kincade wore a wide ammunition bandoleer securing .45-caliber Colt cartridges and central-fire solid-head Winchester Rifle Model 1873 .44-caliber bullets. The cartridge belt went up and over his left shoulder, down to his right hip, and back up again. The bandoleer was now caked with dried blood from Logan's bullet wound.

On his feet he wore mule-eared boots, pants tucked in, and bibbed spurs with harness snaps and two-and-a-quarter-inch rowels and jingle bobs to keep Gold Digger happy.

Kincade swung up into the Texas cattle-drover slick-fork, arching his right leg to just clear the high-backed cantle, slipping his knee beneath a twenty-five-foot riata, held fast to the saddle with an eight-inch strip of worn latigo. He jammed both boots into tapaderos.

Gold Digger stood patiently as Kincade produced a worn pair of gloves that had been tucked within the saddle's open gullet. Both were long since missing the entire first leather digit of thumb and trigger finger from jerking and firing the pistols with blazing speed. Kincade slowly pulled the gloves on, flexing his fingers fully out, then back into a palm knot, and out once more. Then he picked up the two braided bridle reins in his right hand.

Kincade moved his left hand to his chest, just center of his heart, and fingered the old Indian's medicine bag, suspended by a strap that ran around his neck. He touched the beaded circle. As he had done countless times, Kincade wondered what the strange leather patch inside meant. The morning young Kincade had been sold for a second-hand rifle and a jug of whiskey, the old Indian said that the bag and its contents were the key to a big secret.

It was a mystery. The answer to the puzzle would come, someday, at some place. Kincade was sure of that.

Kincade looked toward the southwestern horizon. Logan and his bunch would soon learn that Kincade hadn't been killed or captured during the stage robbery. They would know that he would be after them. As cunning as Logan was, Kincade knew exactly where to go. Scum that Logan was, Kincade knew he would use Josephine for bait.

So be it.

Running his right hand over his mustache, he spurred the pale horse forward. Beneath his breath and nearly inaudible, as though a ghost were whispering in the wind, Kincade mouthed four words:

"You'll get yours, Logan . . ."

6

Melissa Wilcox's favorite thing to do was to go into Julesburg with Papa. She was certain that the nicest people in the whole world lived there. Many of them called her Missy, and others by flattering names. "Well, there's Little Miss Sunshine." "How's my sweetheart today?" "Give me a kiss, pretty little lady." If anyone said, "My, you've grown taller than when you were here last time," she would remind them, "I'm going on seven, you know." They were all her friends, and Papa told her to give everyone her sparkling smile and to say thank you. Melissa never met a person she didn't like, and Jethro was as proud as punch. Yes, Melissa was not only the apple of Jethro's eye, but of Julesburg's as well.

They always had much to do in town. Melissa would put on her Sunday best, even if it was Tuesday. While she only had two dresses, she always put on her best one. And hook and eye shoes. And a yellow smock with two big pockets on the front. One pocket held three buttons, a mostly eaten piece of hard candy, and a marble. The other held her most precious possession: Dolly. It was just big enough to sit in her pocket and look out the top. Dolly had big blue eyes and soft red hair—what was left of it. In honor of going to

Julesburg today, Melissa had tied a purple ribbon on the top-knot. The doll's yellow smock matched Melissa's. Frayed bloomers peeked from beneath the tiny hemline. Worn ivory stockings and black shoes with miniature straps completed the outfit. Melissa thought Dolly was beautiful.

On this particular day, as Jethro visited the Julesburg post office, Melissa recalled the day they had mailed the small package with Lena's curl and snippet of dress to the widow Dye in California. "She was a very nice lady, Papa, and I felt so sorry for her. Do you think she ever got it?"

"I hope so. She loved her little girl almost as much as I love you." Melissa giggled and squeezed his hand.

They went to the bank, the general store, and the livery stable. At noon Jethro got Melissa a sarsaparilla in the new cafe and himself a beer in the saloon. They sat on the buckboard and ate their lunch of cheese and bread and apples they had brought with them. Then they went to the schoolhouse to return the lessons Melissa had finished and to pick up new ones. Jethro was teaching her at home.

"You have such a bright little girl, Mr. Wilcox," the schoolmarm cooed. "And so pretty too."

"Thank you. Come along, Melissa. I still have one more errand. Good-bye, Miss Simpson." When Melissa looked back she saw the spinster waving and smiling ear to ear.

"I think Miss Simpson is sweet on you, Papa. Do you like her?"

"I think she is a very proper lady, and I'm all for proper. But I'm only sweet on you."

"Oh Papa, you're funny. I think she looks like a horse."

"Melissa! You mustn't make fun of the way people look."

"Sorry."

"She can't help it if God gave her the teeth of a horse."

They both burst out laughing, and Jethro even whinnied.

It was almost time to return home. Jethro pulled the buckboard in front of the assayer's office. "Do you suppose you're big enough to wait here for just a minute? I need to get some papers."

"Of course, Papa. I'm going on seven, you know."

"You stay right in the buckboard and don't talk to anyone you don't know."

"Yes, Papa. But I know everyone, don't I?"

"Of course you do. I won't be but a minute."

Melissa folded her hands in her lap and looked around. She hummed a little tune and tapped her feet.

The seamstress, Miss Mason, waved at her from across the street and then advanced to the buckboard. "Hello, dear. You here all alone?"

"Papa's in the assay office. I'm to wait right here."

"Such a big girl to be left alone. Will he be long?"

"Oh probably."

"Well, you tell him I asked about him and that you and I had this nice little chat. Good-bye, dear." She gave Melissa a molasses smile, adjusted her parasol, and walked on. She looks like a monkey, Melissa thought. A monkey with a parasol . . . that's funny. And she giggled to herself. Papa was taking too long, and she began to fidget. Waiting was not her favorite thing to do. She took Dolly from her pocket and instructed the toy on the correct manners of waiting and greeting people.

Then Melissa saw a huge man she didn't know. He was staring at her. "That's very rude," she said to Dolly. "He should either say hello or move along." He was not a very nice-looking man. He wore a dirty black duster and full batwing chaps. His ugly face was a rough red color, and there was tobacco spit in his shaggy beard. He grinned at Melissa, and his teeth were yellow and cracked. Melissa squirmed and turned away. She put Dolly back in her pocket so the ugly man wouldn't frighten her. She hoped Papa would hurry.

When Jethro climbed aboard the buckboard she threw her arms around him. "Well, well. To what do I owe this treat?"

"I just love you so much, Papa." She snuggled up to him as they set off down the road out of town.

Melissa was unusually quiet. Should she tell Papa about that man? She decided not to. He was probably just a drifter or maybe someone off a wagon train headed for Oregon.

"What's on your mind, my angel? You're usually chattering like a magpie."

She thought quickly. "I've been working on a new plan to catch that fat fish that swims in the eddy by the big rock. Maybe I'll try it when we get home if you'll let me."

"Do you promise we'll have him for dinner?"

"Papa! I don't want to eat him . . . just catch him. I'll show that fish I can do anything I want to. And then I'll throw him back in the water. Won't he be surprised?"

"Won't you be surprised if your new plan works? If I remember correctly you've been trying to catch that fish for three months."

"But this is a special plan that's guaranteed to work." And the thought of how to catch the fish so occupied her mind that she forgot all about the ugly man who had stared at her.

As the two arrived home, she hopped down from the buckboard, and Jethro warned, "Don't be long at the creek, Melissa. You have chores to do before dinner. And keep that red sunbonnet on so I can see where you are."

"Okay, Papa." She waved at her father and blew him a kiss so tender, so heartfelt, that Jethro felt tears well up.

Melissa had figured it all out on the way home. If she

came at that slippery fish with the sun to her back, the trout wouldn't see her. She had tried everything else. Then she would just lower her hand slowly into the water, and grab that big fat trout before he knew what was coming. After that, she would yank him from the water, hold him up to her face where he could get a good look at her, and do what she had been planning for all these months. She would stick her tongue out at him, and waggle it around a little. "That'll show that fish who's boss!" she said to herself. She took Dolly out of her pocket and propped her against a rock. "You sit there and watch me, because you mustn't fall in the water."

And so, that's exactly what she was doing: sneaking up on one big fat trout. Today was the day.

Melissa crept to the edge of the riverbank, crouching down low. She stepped carefully onto the big flat rock in the shallow waters. The sun was squarely at her back, all ablaze, setting the water on fire. Suddenly she was covered by a large shadow. She thought a cloud had sprung up. That happened sometimes. She would just have to move over a little. All she needed to do was turn around, see where that cloud was, move a step this way or that, and the big fat fish was hers.

She twisted around and looked up. Five very big men on the biggest horses she had ever seen were quietly waiting on the riverbank. They were all watching her. In the middle of the five was the ugly man she had seen in town. His eyes were as cold as a dead snake.

Melissa knew her smile usually charmed everyone, so she smiled even if she didn't feel like it. "Howdy to you all. My name's Melissa, and I'm going on seven years old."

They didn't move. The creek burbled, and a slight breeze momentarily ruffled the little girl's smock.

For some reason, her skin began to crawl. The ugly man opened his greasy mouth and hissed, "Well, Melissa, my name's Wil Logan, and I'm older than God." The other four guffawed.

Then silence.

Melissa knew something was wrong—more wrong than anything she had ever experienced in her entire life. She bit her lower lip, took a deep breath, and stammered, "I'm trying to catch this fish." She pointed her finger with shaken confidence at the sparkling water. "He's a good fish, I think. And pretty soon, I'll show him that he better not wrestle with me. I'm a good fisher."

Silence.

She tried to swallow, but her mouth had become completely dry. One of the horses shook its withers from the vampire bite of a horsefly. No one moved. Five sets of bloodshot eyes were locked onto little Melissa.

Then, without warning, Logan slowly swung from his saddle, and moved toward Melissa. He was a huge man. His spurs made a menacing sound as he approached.

Melissa forgot all about the fish. She suddenly flashed on her Papa's loving face and the chores she had promised to do before supper. She tried to run, and her sunbonnet fell off. She tripped over Dolly, who fell into the water.

Logan was fast. He swept her into his arms, crushed her to his chest, walked back to his mount, slammed Melissa behind the cantle, and climbed into the saddle. Melissa whimpered. Logan reached a filthy paw around and slapped her face hard.

"God, Logan, why you want to take a snivelin' brat with us?" one of his riders complained.

But another chortled, "Maybe she's our reward for doin' such a fine job robbin' that Wells Fargo stage."

The idea caught on. They all whooped. "Leaving Kincade in the dirt with a front-row ticket to his own necktie party was just about the finest piece 'a work we've ever done."

"You gonna give us each a turn with the kid to show your appreciation, Logan?"

Logan put his finger alongside his right nostril, inhaled deeply, and blew a glob of snot onto the ground. "Shut up and ride. When I want you to know my reason for anything I'll tell you."

Logan yanked little Melissa's hair up so the pack of wolves on horseback could see her terrified eyes. "You're lookin' at an ace up my sleeve!"

Five very big men on five very big horses turned from the stream and galloped southwest. Now, there was a very small, and very frightened, sixth companion. Logan had a plan for the girl that was very different from the one his gang suspected. It wasn't the first time he had kept things from his own men. And it wouldn't be the last. Logan only cared about one thing—killing Kincade—and this trophy was going to help.

As twilight descended and Melissa hadn't returned, Jethro Wilcox called for his daughter. When no answer came, he frantically went searching, stumbling over stones, crashing through willows with an all-consuming fear he had only felt once before in his life. When he came to the big rock by the eddy, he saw the hoofprints of five large horses. He saw Melissa's red sunbonnet and knelt in the mud to pick it up with trembling fingers. A splash in the water startled him. It was Melissa's trout, leaping to grab a water skipper.

Jethro started to cry.

As the fish disappeared, and the water stilled, Jethro saw a smashed face staring up at him from a liquid grave. It was Melissa's Dolly, once so precious and now so abandoned.

On muddied knees, Jethro crawled to the water's edge and gently picked the doll from beneath the waters. An indescribable terror coursed through his veins as his mind raced, the memories of the Nebraska massacre screaming in his head, ricocheting with what he feared must have happened to Melissa.

The wind suddenly stiffened. The father's ears pricked, listening . . . Was that the far-off scream of his little girl?

Jethro felt destroyed. He knew in his bones that this kidnapping had been done by the same man who murdered his wife in Nebraska. Wil Logan was sent from the inferno below to bring hellfire into his life, not once but twice. He raised his eyes to heaven, searching for some reason innocent settlers, and even more innocent little girls, were killed. He had never felt so empty, so utterly hopeless in his entire life.

The remains of the drowned doll were cradled in his hands. Jethro removed the worn bandana from his left jacket pocket and carefully wrapped the crushed face. He opened several buttons of his flannel shirt, carefully placing Melissa's Dolly inside. He refastened the buttons, making sure that no more harm came to the doll.

Jethro resurrected the image of his little girl, waving good-bye to him a scant few hours before, her pockets cradling three buttons, a piece of candy, a marble, and her precious porcelain doll, giggling about the capture of an evasive trout.

Jethro lowered his head to the ground as a primeval wail arose from somewhere very deep within him. Jethro Wilcox cried even harder than he had when his wife Emily was taken from him on the Nebraska plains.

7

Young Kincade made a vow that night in his seventeenth year, as he recovered in the livery shed struggling for breath, knowing he had nearly been killed by Logan's knife. "I'm gonna learn to save my life with guns. I vow never to give Logan—or any man like him—a second chance."

He looked for work away from town. He was going to miss Jesse, but he knew Wil would kill him sooner or later if he didn't leave. When he got hired on as a ranch hand, he met with Jesse for the last time.

"You want my cache of stuff, Jess?"

"Ain't you gonna need it?"

Kincade shook his head. "I'm gonna be movin' around. I've kept what I need." The two teenagers stood there, not knowing what else to say, or how to say it. Jesse took his right thumb and ran it along his lower lip. Then, he unbuttoned his cuffed shirt and rolled up the sleeve, revealing the scarred incisions made by the doctor the night Kincade's throat had been stitched. "Blood brothers, Kincade. Forever and ever." And as much as it meant to Jesse to be strong, to stay strong, to show his lifelong friend that he was a man, Jesse's eyes filled with tears. The fifteen-year-old boy spun and ran down the street, not wanting Kincade to see how weak he was.

Kincade did many jobs on the ranch. Every free minute was spent perfecting his shooting skills with a gun that one of the wranglers loaned him. When he was a boy, the old Indian had taught him a lot about shooting with a rifle, but never with a pistol and never with a target that could be shooting back. His draw became quick, his aim infallible.

The wrangler watched his progress over many months. "Damn, Kincade. If this ranchin' don't work out for you, you can join Wil Logan's gang."

Kincade's eyes narrowed with anger. "He's got a gang now?"

"Said to be formin' one up. But I hardly think you're his type."

Had that wrangler suggested the opposite, the two of them would have gotten into one hell of a fight. As he grew older Kincade went on roundups and cattle drives as far away as New Mexico, Wyoming, and Montana. There were two kinds: the fall drive took the beef to a railhead for sale to the army or Eastern buyers; the spring drive moved the herd north to seasonal pastures and the maturing of the calves. Ranchers had homesteads in both locations. After a drive, a cowboy could work on the ranch tending to summer or winter chores, or go his own way for other work until the next season's cattle drive.

Rather than lose a summer's wages the first night in town carousing with the other cowboys, Kincade saved every penny. The vow he had made to himself when he was seventeen required more than words. It required his own guns. Not one, but two .45-caliber Colts. "I'll have them someday, I swear I will."

On the cattle drives, Kincade always preferred riding

drag. He had learned that the top hands were to be found there, and only there, because it was the toughest work. Hours into days, into weeks, the herd smashed through sage, kicking up red earth. The wranglers on point and flank guided the herd. But it was the boys on drag who drove them all forward.

In the spring drives the calves were so small, so frightened, so used to their birthplace in the winter pastures, filled with sweet grass and water. Now they were thrown into the push north to the summer range. They tired easily after days of being shoved forward, so weak, so sore. Their mamas were lost to them somewhere ahead. The calves called to them, screaming for protection from the rougher cowboys who cracked whips and rattled cans and popped their knotted ropes on their rumps.

Despite the threats from seasoned cowhands to move forward, never backward, mamas who had lost their calves would fight to return to the drag, searching for their bawling babies. These frantic animals would charge any cowboy who dared to confront them, no matter how formidable his mount. Riding drag was tough, dangerous, challenging, and rewarding. It was where Kincade preferred to be.

When the herd was settled for the day and quietly chewing their cuds, the dinner bell would ring, and the tired cowboys would gather round, glad that they hadn't pulled the night watch. Chow could be good or mediocre, but it was never bad. There was one rancher named Sabin who hired Kincade three drives in a row, and Kincade always signed on because Sabin's cook was so great. Most cowboys nicknamed the man who fixed their meals Cookie, but Sabin's guy was called Whiskey Pete. He was a huge hulk of a man, a gentle giant. Indian bread made with corn meal was his specialty, and he served it every meal.

Whiskey Pete had a pard who was liked as much as his bread—a shaggy black pup named Little Blue. Blue's mom had been a noble and hardworking cowdog who spent her whole life deep within the Crow Indian lands in southern Montana. Even the top hands knew that without her the days' work would turn into weeks. For every mile they rode, she would run three—back and forth, up and down, staying mostly on drag.

That was where Whiskey Pete had first met Big Blue, Little Blue's mom. He had signed on with Mr. Sabin for the spring drive and had quickly grown to respect the little four-legged lady.

About halfway into the push north, a second cattle drive came near the Sabin herd. There, in that other drive, was another hardworking cowdog. Except this pooch was a fella. One evening, the fella and the lady took a liking to one another. Near the edge of the firelight, the two decided to get to know each other just about as well as a fella and a lady can.

And wouldn't you know it . . . Big Blue was soon to have Little Blue.

Whiskey Pete remembered the day Little Blue was born. Big Blue had put in another full day of work. But that night, rather than hanging around the campfire listening to the boys tell their stories, swap lies, and recite whatever poetry they had concocted during the day's ride, Big Blue went off by herself, lay down under a juniper tree and into a soft bed of needles. She gently rolled to her side, and began the miracle of birth. Soon, there were six pups with her. The litter was as tiny as squirrels, their eyes closed shut, mewing, rather than barking, knowing that if they stayed close to their mother, all would be well.

And then Whiskey Pete saw the seventh—Little Blue, the

runt of the litter. Gawd almighty, ain't he cute? he thought. Next day, Mama Big Blue was back running with the herd just as fast and long as before. She might have even been better without her belly dragging to the ground. Whiskey Pete cleared out a storage box and put the puppies in the chuck wagon. Several times a day Mama Big Blue would come to check on their welfare and let them nurse. But her job was on drag, and she never remained away long. Each night, as Mama suckled her pups, Whiskey Pete stared wide-eyed, especially at the seventh, his favorite—his Little Blue.

Little Blue got along famously with everyone. But his favorite was Whiskey Pete. It began because of the table scraps thrown Little Blue's way. But it grew because Whiskey Pete was a kind cowboy. His hands may have been rough, but his heart was far bigger than the man himself. Everybody on the ranch loved Whiskey Pete. As long as they didn't get between him and the fire when it was time to prepare the meal, there wasn't anything Pete wouldn't do for them.

Little Blue became Whiskey Pete's dog and no one else's. He was the cook's shadow, and not just because of chuck wagon scraps. The little dog loved the big man. At night the boys would settle around the campfire to smoke and drink Whiskey Pete's black coffee. Little Blue didn't join them even though they would have patted his head and rubbed his tummy. No, Little Blue would stand next to the chuck wagon as if he could help Whiskey Pete wash up the plates and ready the Indian bread for breakfast. If there was time after these chores, the two of them would join the circle, and Little Blue would lay his head on Whiskey Pete's lap.

"Too bad that dog ain't a woman," one cowboy jeered. "You'd have one hell of a lover." Whiskey Pete shot back. "And if you was a bitch in heat, Little Blue would have noth-in' to do with you." All the cowboys clapped and cheered. At the end of that drive, Big Blue's pups were let out of the box to begin their lives as ranch dogs. But Little Blue didn't want to leave Whiskey Pete's side. One evening, Whiskey Pete walked up to Mr. Sabin with his hat in his hand. "Sir, do you suppose it would be alright if I kept Little Blue with me?" The rancher smiled widely. "Of course, Pete. Little Blue's always been your dog." No one could ever remember a breakfast as grand as the one Whiskey Pete proudly prepared that following morning. Little Blue didn't have to settle for scraps that day. The man set the dog his own plate. Kincade might not have understood the bond between Whiskey Pete and Little Blue if he hadn't met an animal that grabbed his heart with the same intensity. It was a tawny palomino named Gold Digger. Kincade's own horse had gone lame just before the drive. Rather than lose a good hand, the rancher stabled Kincade's horse and loaned him one of his prize stallions. Sabin had seen Kincade ride, and anybody who could cowboy like that could more than handle a horse like Gold Digger.

Gold Digger was different from any horse Kincade had ever known. The beast was flat-out handsome, had an enormous chest, with a long silver mane and a tail that ran to near white. But more than that, he was smart. He was a great cutting horse as well as a riding horse. Right from the beginning he understood Kincade's every signal. With a slight pressure of the cowboy's knees or heel, Digger would turn a walk into a gallop, a switch-back into a come-around. It was as if they were speaking the same language. Nothing gave Kincade more peace of mind at the end of a long, hard day than to groom Gold Digger with his bare hands, running them along the palomino's golden coat, one stroke after another, removing burrs and dried dirt, smoothing, caressing, letting the horse know how much he meant to Kincade.

First one side and then the other, repeating each step carefully, with purpose, with the intent of communicating without speaking. Then he would comb the long, blond mane and tail with his fingers, easing the snarls or cutting them out. Gold Digger stood perfectly still. One night Kincade stood squarely in front of the horse, looking straight into the large dark eyes of its massive head. "You're gonna be mine, Gold Digger—if I have to work for Mr. Sabin the rest of my life." The horse nuzzled his cheek. He understood.

That summer at Mr. Sabin's high ranch, Whiskey Pete came to realize that Kincade was pretty much a loner. He kept to himself. Kincade preferred to stay at the edge of the campfire's light, rather than huddled in close like the rest of the outfit. Even so, whenever Whiskey Pete spoke to Kincade, he would have his full attention. The sparkle in Kincade's eyes when Whiskey Pete told a good one made him believe that while Kincade was a loner, he never seemed to be lonely.

No wonder it took Whiskey Pete by surprise when, one day, while he and Kincade were stretched out on a riverbank watching Little Blue frolic in the clear waters, Kincade began to open up, revealing a few bits and pieces of his life. Kincade told Whiskey Pete about having to fend for himself when he was a boy, that he had a good friend named Jesse Keller who was just as bad off, and that they had been as close as brothers. Pete could tell that Kincade missed Jesse, and he wondered why the two had parted ways.

Then, after a long pause, Kincade's voice lowered. He began to talk about another boy named Wil Logan. Listening to Kincade speak, it quickly became clear to Whiskey Pete that this Logan had a bitter hatred for his friend. Kincade had some sort of pull over Logan that drove Wil wild with rage. There was no explaining the reasons why.

Then, Kincade removed the wildrag from his throat and showed Whiskey Pete the scar. "I'd be dead from that wound if Jesse hadn't saved me." Then he told him about becoming blood brothers with his friend. As Kincade spoke, Whiskey Pete realized that no man had ever been that honest or open with him. He knew that Kincade would never open up like that if the man didn't feel deep trust and respect for him. That realization meant more to Whiskey Pete than anything Kincade could ever say with words. He grew to like Kincade a great deal. Whiskey Pete was pretty sure Little Blue did too.

Some Saturdays, Whiskey Pete, Little Blue, and Kincade would ride into a nearby mining camp with the other cowhands. Whiskey Pete learned that Kincade loved a good saloon, even if the one in the camp was no more than a weather-beaten tent. Not so much for the golden tequila Kincade preferred, but because of what Kincade learned about others, and himself, once inside. Whiskey Pete learned that whenever Kincade found himself among people, he would stay back and intently "listen." Not just to the words being spoken, but to what wasn't being said. "It's in their eyes," he would say. "It's always in their eyes." Kincade could literally take measure of men, absorb everything around him, learning, testing, weighing, taking in what could be used to advantage later, and discarding what couldn't, all by looking into their eyes. It was what Kincade called "the Wait."

The bartenders and saloonkeepers for hundreds of miles either knew Kincade personally or had heard of him. The stories of Kincade's tremendous skills with guns had spread. Those same stories brought Kincade a reputation. So whenever he stepped up to a bar, the saloonkeeper knew to pour a generous shot of tequila without so much as being asked.

Whenever Whiskey Pete stood alongside Kincade, the bartender would turn to him and ask, "What's for you?" "Same as him. And my dog would like a bowl 'a beer—makes him sneeze." The summer's ranch work ended, and it came time for Mr. Sabin to settle up with his hands. Kincade headed over to the ranch house early one morning and knocked on the door. "I'd sure like to own Gold Digger, Mr. Sabin. Would you trade that horse for what you owe me?" Actually Kincade's pay was not nearly what the horse was worth. Mr. Sabin hesitated. "My own horse has healed," Kincade added. "You can have him as part of the deal."

Kincade had always been a hard worker, never caused any trouble, and Sabin liked him. "Okay. But you owe me two more drives—gratis." Kincade threw his hat into the air. He had just got the best friend of his life—barring Jesse.

Kincade told Whiskey Pete of his bargain with Mr. Sabin and promised he would be back for the two drives agreed to. They warmly shook hands. Kincade knelt down to scratch behind the ears of Pete's dog. "Little Blue, you good dog you." And if a dog could smile, this one did.

Swinging onto Gold Digger, Kincade spurred the stallion into a full gallop. He had heard of a saloon unlike any other in a town called Benson. And he was going to celebrate.

Kincade loved a good saloon—not the drinking, although he downed his shots with the best of them. He just loved the "act of saloonin'," as he called it. First there was a right way of swinging open the batwings—always together, and just a moment's hesitation before entering. Then came the wealth of nostril pleasures—whiskey, smoke from cigars and rolled cigarettes, cheap perfume—odors that gratified the palate, tempted the soul, and led innocent boys astray. The sounds were intoxicating. Men's loud voices mixed with the plunking of a honky-tonk piano. The lusty laughter of bar belles or their sweet whispers in a cowboy's ear. A big smile crossed his face in anticipation of overflowing libation bottles displayed on the back bar. Kincade could just smell the tequila, with maybe a beer to soothe the burn. Yep, Kincade was ready.

Late that same day, Kincade rode into the town of Benson on Gold Digger with the pride of ownership. On Main Street he stepped off the horse in one easy motion. Kincade whistled to a boy. "Would you please bring my horse some water and let him drink his fill. Then take him to the livery," Kincade directed. "Tell them to feed him well but not to put Gold Digger with any other horse."

"How come?" the boy asked.

Kincade looked at the youngster. "Because he'd probably eat him." The boy's eyes grew wide. Kincade winked, tussled the boy's hair, and reaching into his pocket he flipped a five-dollar gold piece into the kid's hand.

"Gosh, thanks, mister!"

As Kincade started to step up onto the boardwalk he felt a gentle tap on his shoulder. Turning, he looked into the startling eyes of the most spectacularly beautiful woman he had ever seen.

"Hello," she said, in a soft dusky voice.

"Miss," acknowledged Kincade, touching the brim of his hat. He had a habit of doing that. As rough as the gunfighter appeared, and often acted, he simply could not stand disrespect for women. Over the years, and through the camps he had traveled, he knew the unspeakable horrors faced by the women who were trapped there. More than once, Kincade had kicked the teeth out of men who tried to boost their egos by belittling women.

It was with the utmost respect that Kincade silently

admired the striking woman before him. Gold silk hair caressed her shoulders. A comb fanned above her hair, pierced by two pearl needles, each eight inches long. A loose curl caressed each petite ear. They framed an exquisite face, accented by cheeks the color of sweet dairy crème. Her lips—the color of dark rubies—were generous, full, and moist. Her sparkling blue eyes crackled with fire.

Chiseled collarbones swept from her smooth neck, standing sentinel over generous breasts that cradled an ivory brooch within a spectacular testament of crème-colored cleavage that would make even the toughest gunman weep. A red-velvet button-front top parted by physical necessity and then finally tightened ever so beautifully at her sculpted waist. Her arms were covered in a gossamer fabric that reached from above her elbows, down and over her hands, only to end just above her fingers so that her exquisite hands could be admired.

The boardwalk was swept with at least a half-dozen lace petticoats, swathed in a black-velvet skirt, accented with a bustle that attractively graced her curvaceous backside. Kincade could imagine that long legs danced beneath the black-velvet sea, the fabric swishing against her thighs. Her feet were cradled in petite white boots laced with satin ribbons to just above her ankles—or at least Kincade assumed they reached above her ankles.

The lady was framed by a white-lace parasol that rested on her left shoulder, opening like a white rose behind her angelic face. Gawking gentlemen who were in Benson for the first time stood mesmerized at the corner of the boardwalk, forgetting that their cigar ashes were burning holes in their vests.

She offered her right hand to Kincade, who took it lightly within his own, raising it to kiss ever so respectfully. The slight scent of jasmine perfume filled his head.

"My name is Josephine. I own the Proud Cat Dance Hall and Saloon," she said demurely, pointing down the street. "Would you be so kind as to help me carry a few packages to my room? I've just returned on the stage from a trip to San Francisco, and I seem to have bought more than I can manage."

"Of course, miss. My name is Kincade, and I would be happy to oblige. I was about to enter your establishment, so carrying your purchases would be a pleasure." He walked to the stagecoach, which was drawn up in front of the Proud Cat. "Which of these boxes are yours?"

"All of them. But my boy will bring in the largest ones. Just choose the hat boxes and that one green carpet bag." Kincade picked them off the stage, grabbing two hatboxes in each hand and stuffing the bag under his arm. "You're very kind," she said with a warm smile. "Please follow me."

"A pleasure, miss." And he thought, A real pleasure.

Kincade followed her into the Proud Cat where she was greeted with shouts of joy followed by hugs and kisses. "May I gather your bags, Miss Josie?" the bartender asked.

"No thank you, Finley. This gentleman is carrying my most precious ones, and I'll send for the others when I'm settled. Please follow me, Mr. Kincade."

"It's just Kincade, miss—no 'mister.'"

"Very well, Kincade it is."

They ascended a stairway leading to a balcony above the Proud Cat and stopped at the first door. She made no effort to unlock it. "Shall I put them inside, miss?"

"No, you may leave the boxes here in the hallway," she said, and then added, "I think it might be wise if you first treated yourself to a bath and a shave." She gave him a tantalizing smile. "If you can manage to do that in an hour, come back and one of my ladies might be interested in teaching you how to Dance." She winked at him, opened the door, and stepped inside.

Kincade's eyes opened wide, and a smile crossed his face. If the Dance had anything to do with that wink, then the tune would probably be set to the rhythmic squeaking of bedsprings.

While the thought certainly caught his attention, Kincade was more curious about the lady of the house. How had someone so beautiful ended up in Benson? After only moments in her presence, Kincade knew that Josephine was not only a true lady, but that she had an inner power that could only have come by walking through fire and emerging with the strength of steel.

For the next two days, Kincade enjoyed his share of mescal, poured generously by the Proud Cat's saloonkeeper Finley, whose use of proper language and etiquette suggested an education that far surpassed the skills necessary to tend bar. As was his nature, Kincade kept pretty much to himself. The years of being alone had honed him into the man he had become. Alone, but never lonely.

On the third day, after checking on the welfare of Gold Digger, Kincade found Mr. Sabin and his wranglers in the Proud Cat, gambling, drinking, and laughing with Josephine's girls.

"Glad to see you, Kincade," Mr. Sabin said. "We're pulling out tomorrow."

"If it's all the same to you, I think I'll stay in Benson this winter."

"Your choice. But don't forget you owe me two drives, and I expect one of them this spring when we move the beef north."

"You can count on me."

"What ya gonna do in Benson?" one of the boys asked. "Gamble till you're broke?"

"Or drink yourself stupid?" put in another.

Kincade didn't answer as his eyes were locked on to the spectacular proprietor of the Proud Cat, who was at that very moment fluttering a tortoise shell and ostrich feather fan as she welcomed three cowpokes into her saloon. "Hello, boys," he heard Josephine say, offering her hand as the trio quickly doffed their hats in respect. Even from across the room, Kincade could hear her silks and satins swish like gentle wind in tall grass.

"Hey, Kincade, you deaf or somethin'?" someone asked, and the hands laughed as they noticed the object of Kincade's attention.

"Boys, I'll level with you," Kincade smiled. "I'm hopin' to talk the lady of this house into giving me Dancin' lessons."

8

The four months that Kincade spent in Benson were a revelation to him. It all started the third week after Sabin and his men had left town.

Kincade had taken a room at the hotel next to the Proud Cat Dance Hall and Saloon. His days were consumed on the prairie, honing his considerable skills with pistols, and competing with Gold Digger to see just who was better: the rider or the horse.

Each night, after a thorough bath and fifteen minutes with a straight razor, Kincade would find himself in the Proud Cat Dance Hall and Saloon. Patrons who came from the street through the batwing doors knew immediately that the Proud Cat was unlike any other establishment in Benson.

There was hardwood instead of sawdust on the floor. Gaslights brightly flickered. The bar stretched nearly the length of the saloon with a large mirrored back bar. The imported libations were tiered row upon row, tempting and pleasing the most discriminating thirst. Those who had no such tastes could request Indian whiskey, which was the best of the brews distilled on the back lots of Benson.

At the back of the saloon a staircase led to an open second-floor balcony with a rail to make sure that Josephine's guests didn't inadvertently launch themselves into the crowd below. Here were five small rooms and Josie's large suite. Two were kept for her ladies' use should some friend be found worthy of the more intimate entertainment of the Dance. Josephine would reserve the three other rooms for a variety of purposes. Private big-stakes poker games were played in them. Business deals could be consummated in a pleasant and quiet atmosphere. Lands were bought and sold, mining claims were challenged and resolved, information on the breeding and selling of cattle was exchanged, even matters of inheritance were laid on the table in these rooms. And of course there was just the pleasure of Josephine's ladies bringing refreshments to a select clientele.

Rarely a woman's presence would be required at a meeting, and Josephine did her best to put the lady at ease. She would greet the lady at the batwings and escort her up the stairs, chatting amicably about the woman's children, church work, and the rising price of victuals. She would offer tea while the men had their liquor. When the meeting ended she would be there to escort the lady down the stairs, suggesting that perhaps they could meet some time at the new coffeehouse. Josephine was so genuine, so gracious, so caring that all women felt respect in her presence.

The real action of the Proud Cat took place in the man's world on the main floor. On one side of the saloon was a small stage complete with a painted backdrop of an ancient Roman villa. Here a honky-tonk piano player tickled the pearly eighty-eights all through the night. The face of the piano stood open so patrons could see the keys striking hundreds of wires singing out like there was no tomorrow.

Four times each night the eight ladies of the Proud Cat

Dance Hall and Saloon would discontinue serving drinks and mount the stage to entertain with singing and dancing. Sometimes it was a soloist, sometimes a line of lovelies, and the piano player might add his lusty voice. There was a varying degree of talent, but the patrons were hushed during the performance, and the applause was always thunderous. After their act the ladies would come around to the tables and invite men of their choosing to trip the light fantastic with them on the dance floor that occupied the center of the room.

Josephine's ladies wore costumes that would drop any cowboy in his tracks. They usually wore their hair piled on top of their heads, with small pearl fans or ivory needles holding their locks in place. Sparkling necklaces were at their throats. Their ample bosoms were tucked into formfitting satin and silk corsets in reds, greens, and blues, cut low enough at the neckline so that most cowboys never even noticed their flashy jewelry. At the edge of their corsets, two inches of tassel fringe danced as they moved through the crowd. They wore silk stockings, textured with a slight black mesh. All in all, a man could end up a blithering idiot in the company of women such as these, for Josephine chose her girls with great care. They had to be strong yet gentle, beautiful because of who they were, and who they wished to be, engaging and thoroughly enjoyable companions—in conversation, in laughter, and many times in love.

Josephine treated the people who worked for her as graciously as those who spent their wages there. Each had her respect from the moment she hired them, and the only way they could lose Josie's high opinion would be of their own doing. Josephine gave people the benefit of the doubt from the start.

Josephine expected her ladies to have respect for her

guests. And Josephine got respect for the ladies themselves. If any stranger got out of line with one of the ladies, three dozen incensed men wouldn't hesitate to educate him on proper manners with a proper woman. They would enlighten the fellow on the street outside the Proud Cat. "Look, laugh, talk, enjoy all you want, cowboy," they would explain. "But don't touch a Proud Cat lady unless you're invited. If you want a whore, go down to the end of the street. Understand?"

Night after night, Kincade kept to himself, immersed in the Wait. But those evenings weren't spent taking the measure of men, but rather watching Josephine. She had an uncanny ability to make every person she met feel like they were the most important in her life. It revolved around her ability to listen. When others spoke, she didn't just pay them polite lip service. She didn't stare off into the distance, or over their shoulders to see if someone else more important deserved her attention. Her deep-water eyes could find the good in most, and the bad in some. It struck Kincade that the lady genuinely cared about people, about those who worked with her, about those who entered her saloon and entered her life. She attracted and mesmerized all those around her like intoxicating nectar. It wasn't just her long blond hair or her ruby red lips. It was something deep within her. People could feel it when she looked at them.

Each evening as Kincade leaned against the Proud Cat bar, sipping the golden tequila poured by Finley, he would watch Josephine work her magic. And as those evenings came and went, Kincade noticed that Josephine began looking at him. Maybe it was just a quick smile, or a slight wave from a gloved hand, but Josephine noticed him more and more. He was sure of it. Josephine's eyes had the power to melt a man's heart, no matter how tough he thought he was. "It was always in the eyes."

As the end of his first month in Benson neared, Kincade and the barkeep Finley had developed a comfortable relationship. Kincade liked the fact that Finley didn't ask too many questions. Finley appreciated the same discretion from Kincade, and as a result, it didn't surprise either one of them when one night Kincade asked Finley a very personal question, or that Finley would reply in such an open and honest manner.

"Good evening, Kincade," Finley smiled as he turned to the back bar, selecting his finest bottle of mescal, picking a freshly washed shot glass, blowing the dust from the bottom just to make sure, placing it before Kincade, and filling it to the brim.

"Evening, Finley."

Without being asked, Finley poured a frothy glass of beer, placing it next to the shot glass. Kincade turned and looked across the saloon, immediately seeing Josephine laughing with a table full of cowhands, producing a fresh desk of cards from her bodice, handing it to their faro dealer with a wink, making the cowhands laugh all the harder.

Kincade turned back to Finley, looked into the man's eyes, then down at the bar, made a decision, glanced back up, and spoke. "Tell me about her."

Finley smiled slightly. "The way you two have been looking at one another, I was beginning to wonder why you hadn't asked me a few weeks ago." Kincade smiled in return. "Mr. Kincade, I sincerely hope your speed with those pistols exceeds the time it has taken you to explore the mysteries of our sweet Josephine." Kincade laughed.

"You asked, and it is my distinct pleasure to answer." And Finley began.

"Josie used to run a stagecoach station on the Cherokee Trail. Quite isolated in that untamed land, life at the station was achingly hard. But our Josephine's courage made her place a vital stop on America's westward journey. Prairie travelers from hundreds of miles would come to Josie's. They'd sit for a spell, enjoy her food and drink, hear her laugh, and watch her rather engaging blue eyes. Our Josephine is extremely beautiful, wouldn't you agree, Mr. Kincade?"

No argument from Kincade on that score.

"That's where my family and I first met Josephine," continued Finley. Kincade was surprised at this reference to family, as he had always seen Finley alone. "Our stage had stopped at her establishment for the evening. My wife Louisa and our sixteen-year-old son Joshua were very taken by her. Josie offered each of us work: I as her bartender, Louisa as keeper of her rooms, and Joshua with whatever chores she needed done."

With those words, Finley suddenly stopped. Kincade could see the man deliberately swallow. He pursed his lips, and blinked. "Just a moment, if you would, sir." Finley curled the fingers of his right hand into his palm, and brought it to cover his mouth. He looked down, swallowed again, staying absolutely silent for what must have been more than two minutes. Kincade didn't move, or speak. Finally, Finley removed his hand and returned to look at Kincade.

"Josephine's station lay just outside a rather coarse, windblasted West Texas town that seemed like a powder keg waiting to explode. And one winter, it did.

"A band of the greediest, meanest cutthroats north of the Baja, savage bandits who made killing their business, burned Josephine's place to the ground." Kincade reeled. "They were led by a vicious and heartless piece of gutter trash, bent on bringing horror into the lives of anyone, or anything, he touched.

"Miss Josie and I had taken the buggy into town for provisions, leaving my wife and son to prepare for the arrival of the noon stage and that evening's guests."

Finley's voice lowered, but he was determined to finish what he had begun. "These men tied my wife and son to a beam. They set the whole place ablaze. The timbers were so dry, the station turned into a hellfire. That day I lost everything I loved." His right hand returned to cover his mouth as his left hand cleared the tears now welling in both his eyes. "I'm sorry."

Kincade reached out his left hand, taking Finley's arm to comfort him. "Finley, I'm . . . "

"It was years ago, Kincade."

"Who did this?"

"I don't know his name. A vicious dog.

"If it hadn't been for Miss Josie, I would have taken my own life. But she helped me understand that my wife and son would want me to go on, that their memory deserved to go on through me. And she was correct." Finley reached into the left front pocket of his vest, producing a golden locket about the size of a pocket watch. He pushed the crown on top, and it opened. He held it out to Kincade, who could see small pictures of a proud young boy and an even prouder woman. Kincade nodded.

"After a proper burial, Miss Josie and I came here. To Benson." Finley looked into Kincade's eyes. "She's quite unusual, Kincade. Her kindness, her spirit, her caring for others is stronger than the awesome power of the high desert, be it good or bad." He paused. "I know."

Finley smiled, having recovered from what must have been an incredibly difficult few moments. "If you'll excuse me, Mr. Kincade. I believe the gentleman at the other end of the bar wishes another round."

Kincade nodded, watching Finley tend to his thirsty customer. After a few moments of considering what he had just heard, he turned back to continue the Wait.

A table of young cattle drovers was having a high time

spending every cent they had earned over the past two months. One young cowboy heard the swish of a floor-length gown and felt a hand on his shoulder. Startled, the eighteen-year-old cattle drover tensed so hard he nearly cracked the molar in the right rear of his jaw.

"Hello, cowboy. Thanks for dropping in. I bet you've ridden a long way, and I'm glad you've come to the Proud Cat. My ladies will be performing in about a half-hour. In the meantime, is there anything I can do to make your evening a memorable one?"

The young cowboy looked up from his chair and into the most beautiful eyes he had ever seen. The bluest of blues, dancing, warm, and totally inviting, haloed by an angelic face framed by cascading waterfalls of blond hair with the sheen of corn silk. His heart literally stopped.

"My name is Josephine," she said. "And this is my saloon." She smiled to all seated around the table, offering her hand to the young cowboy. He jumped out of his chair, immediately doffed his buckaroo hat, revealing about four inches of cowlick. He was wide-eyed and agog. Only an hour before, he and the other cowboys had finished penning their West Texas herd in the rail yards just south of town. The foreman then released the hands after giving them their eight weeks' wages. He had gotten a room, splashed enough water on his body to get most of the dust off, and headed to the Proud Cat Dance Hall and Saloon. And now, this stunning woman—the owner herself!— was welcoming all of them as though they were the mayor and town council. She seemed genuinely happy to have them there.

"Thank you, ma'am," he stuttered. He felt so odd being treated with such respect, certainly by a total stranger, most certainly by someone like Josephine. Yet, the way she spoke to him, her ease, her presence, made him feel like he had known her since the day he was born. A real lady, standing right alongside his chair, actually talking to him.

"May I freshen your drink?" she offered. "We want all of you to feel welcome here, so I hope you enjoy our little show."

The rest of the drovers jumped from their seats, quickly removing their hats in unison. Never in their lives had they been made to feel this way about themselves.

Only one thing kept going through the eighteen-year-old's mind. He blurted out, "Boy howdy, do you smell good!" Josie laughed. "Please, take your seats, gentlemen. Enjoy yourselves. Let us know if there's anything you need." They did, they were, and they would.

Josephine smiled and strolled to the adjacent table to visit with a local rancher. She listened attentively as he shared how his children were growing and that his oldest boy would probably take over the ranch soon. She nodded and wished him well, turned to her right, and looked directly at Kincade. She smiled and nodded her head to him ever so slightly.

Kincade reached his right hand to the brim of his hat, touching the edge lightly, and nodded back. He had never in his life felt anything like what coursed though his heart at that very moment. He had never had a relationship with a woman. He had never had a mother that he knew of, no sister, no aunt nor cousin, not even a female friend. Something was happening deep within him. Something he had never felt before.

Finley could see it in Kincade's eyes. "It was always in the eyes . . ."

9

The two-inch round branch over the dry creek bed was squarely in the sights of Kincade's Winchester 73. From one hundred yards and with three quick jerks of the lever action, Kincade blew the branch into a trio of chunks before the first piece hit the ground.

He had to think. Thoughts of Josephine had filled his head over the last week in ways that made the preceding month pale in comparison.

Setting the rifle down, Kincade unhooked the leather tie-downs from twin-rig Colt holsters. Without blinking, Kincade skinned both smoke wagons, his thumbs cocking the hammers before the barrels began to clear the leather, firing one then two bullets into a discarded bean can forty feet away, sending it up, cocking and recocking, firing and firing again with such blazing speed that the can continued to jerk up and up with each successive impact, making it appear that the tin must be attached to the sky by invisible marionette strings. In less than four seconds, all twelve rounds were spent as Kincade swirled in the gunsmoke, reholstering both six-shooters with a three-revolution snap of the wrists. Gold Digger stood patiently, indifferent to this blazing display of gunplay.

Kincade remembered that the old Indian had told him there were two ways to figure out your feelings for a woman. Neither one of them worked.

"Ahem."

Kincade nearly jumped out of his skin, spinning on the loose gravel at the voice ten feet behind his back, nearly tripping himself in the process.

"You know, Kincade," whispered Josephine, "for someone who is so quiet when he looks at me, you're certainly making a lot of noise." And she looked at him with mischievous aquamarine eyes.

Kincade smiled back. "You distracted me."

"I believe that may have begun some time ago." And once again, she looked deep within him through those amazing eyes.

Kincade silently admitted to himself that was true.

"I was on a walk," she said. "But I hear there are dangerous gunfighters practicing their marksmanship in the creek beds of Benson, and I wondered if you would be so kind to escort me safely home." Again, the smile. And those glorious eyes.

He knelt to pick up the rifle. "What do you say, Digger?"

Large brown eyes looked at Kincade, then at Josephine, then back again. The stallion pawed the ground.

"He wants to know if you can manage his saddle."

Josephine handed her parasol to Kincade, stepped over to Digger, raised her skirt to just above her left knee, and easily swung into the slick fork with the grace of a lynx. She smoothed her six layers of lace petticoats as she gently wiggled back into the cantle. "Tell Digger I'll try."

Kincade smiled, moved in front and to the right of the stallion, sliding the barrel of his rifle deep into the saddle's scabbard. "Room for me up there?"

"I think so," Josephine said. "But it might be tight."

Kincade walked around, stepped into the tapaderos, and swung his right leg over the saddle's skirt, coming to rest just behind the cantle's rise. He reached both hands around Josephine, took the braided reins in his right, placing his left hand on Josephine's waist. "Too tight?" he asked.

"Uh-uh." Kincade caught the slightest scent of her jasmine perfume.

"Ready?"

"Uh-huh." And she ever so slightly snuggled back into his arms. "Kincade . . ."

Kincade felt his head begin to swim deliriously. "Yes?"

"May I please have my parasol?"

During the ride into Benson, neither one spoke. But the two of them said more to one another than in all of the previous six weeks combined. At the hitching post outside the Proud Cat, Kincade slid down from Gold Digger and then reached back up and lifted Josephine from the saddle. He gently lowered her, and as her feet touched the ground, the two of them found their bodies touching. Kincade realized that his hands could easily circle her petite waist.

"Thank you," she said softly.

He was lost in her unbelievably beautiful eyes. "Josie, Finley told me what happened with . . ."

She took her right forefinger and gently touched Kincade's lips, as if she already knew everything he wanted to tell her, and that she wished to assure him that she was all right. "That was then. This is now."

She smiled, and Kincade released her waist. She stepped onto the boardwalk, turned back to Kincade, smiled again, looking at him without saying anything, and because of it, saying everything. She walked inside, leaving Kincade in the street.

"Hey, mister." For the second time that day, Kincade nearly jumped out of his skin.

"You want me to take your horse?" asked the eager stable boy. "I have a stall all ready for him. By hisself."

"Yeah, I would," said Kincade, tossing the boy a gold piece. Except this time, it was worth ten dollars.

"Wow, thanks," he said. "You must be havin' a good day."

Kincade could never recall hearing such an understatement.

As the boy led Gold Digger to his stall for the night, Kincade made a decision that changed the rest of his life. He moved up onto the boardwalk, went into the Proud Cat, walked across its lobby and up the staircase to Josephine's room. He paused, took a deep breath, and knocked on her door.

The latch opened. "Would you like to ask me something, Kincade?" she asked softly.

"Yes." And he looked into those deep blue eyes. "May I have this Dance?"

10

The days and nights that followed were beyond anything Kincade could have possibly imagined. Their love was fiery, explosive, unbridled, insane—for both of them. Neither could get enough. Gradually their passion changed into tenderness. The Dance was an exchange of longing to fulfill each other. It became companionship, listening, understanding, consolation, satisfying needs beyond lust.

Kincade and Josephine talked openly about their pasts. She talked about her family, and the devastation they faced during the Civil War. He told her about Jesse in such depth that Josie felt like she knew him personally. They spoke of Finley, his family, and the fire. Over her life, Josephine had taken very few Dancing partners, and those only for financial security or protection from enemies. When she saw Kincade, she knew true desire for the first time.

Once when they were lying naked and spent she fingered the beaded medicine bag that hung around his neck.

"Why do you always wear that Indian medicine bag—even when we're Dancing?"

"As distracting as you are, Josie, I might lose it or leave it behind. It's very important to me."

Then he told her more about his childhood, surprising her by the news of his upbringing at the hands of the old Indian, and of two great secrets held by the bag. "One is his Indian secret on the outside. The other is mine on the inside. I don't know what this circle of beads means, but I'm sure it has some sort of Indian symbolism. And there's the other part of the secret I haven't learned yet."

He opened the bag and took out the scrap of leather, now turning brittle with age. She took it and carefully examined both sides. "The designs are similar but slightly different, aren't they?"

"Can you make out a 'K' on this side?" he asked her. "I believe that stands for Kincade."

"Yes, and you have it on your arm too." She turned over the leather, touching the five lines; the first four linked like a lightning bolt, and the fifth line standing by itself.

"That's the other part of the secret I have yet to learn."

She put it back in the bag. "Are you curious what it means?"

"Yes, but the answer will come to me—I can't seek it out." He got out of bed and started to dress.

"Why do you wear all the weaponry? It takes so long to put it on." She laughed. "And to take it off."

"'Cause I'm a show-off. I like to look like a bandito."

"Well, you look more like a ban-dodo. I've only seen you shoot tin cans. Did you ever kill anybody?"

Kincade's brow furrowed as if this was a subject he would rather avoid. But Josie seemed to have a way of bringing out the truth in people. "There've been a few rustlers, and bandits, and Indians. And I've backed up a pard or two when I believed they were in the right."

"You've never had an enemy?"

"Just one, and if it ever comes to a showdown between him and me, I guess I could kill him."

"Who is he?"

"You've seen the scar on my neck. It was given me by a man named Wil Logan. He'll come for me one day, I know it."

"Why?"

"I don't know why, but he'll come." He told her all about Wil Logan and the nightmare. "I must be ready for him because one of us is going to die. You can see his picture on the wanted posters in the post office."

"What's he wanted for?"

"You name it—robbery, murder, rape, sacking, burning. A new poster goes up almost every week."

"I've seen enough of bad men in my life. I think I'll leave the looking to you."

"There are pictures of his four main gang members too."

"Well, I suppose Finley and I will have to look at them next time we go."

"Brace yourself. They are five mean-looking hombres."

Kincade spent his days giving Gold Digger a good workout in the desert. The horse loved to run without having to cut cattle or plow through sage. Kincade continued to practice his considerable shooting and knife-throwing skills. Sometimes Josephine would join him on her black Arabian, Soledad. They would race and then find a shady spot to dismount and quietly admire the world around them.

Kincade also worked in the Proud Cat. He could deal faro and poker, spin the roulette wheel. He watched to assure the honesty of the games of chance. Josephine staked him, and he won considerable money for himself.

Spring came, and Sabin's drovers began to arrive for the drive back to summer's pasture. Kincade was a man of his word, and he had given it to Sabin.

When the morning of that day came, Josephine sat before her dressing table mirror. Kincade stood silently behind her, his eyes on her, her eyes on him. He reached over her right shoulder, picked up her ivory-backed hairbrush. Ever so slowly, he began to brush her long hair. No words. Just the soft sound of the bristles flowing through the waterfalls of corn silk. The morning light wafted through the lace curtains, warming her. She closed her eyes and leaned back. No man had ever combed her hair. Ever.

Too soon, he spoke the four words. "I'll be going, Josie." The room was so still.

"I'm going to miss you." She kept her eyes closed. Tears began to fall from beneath the lids.

Kincade leaned over, replaced the brush, and ever so gently kissed the nape of her neck. He backed up, removed his hat from the stand next to the door, turned the knob, looked back at her one final time, walked through and quietly closed the door behind him.

Kincade had always been a loner but had never seen himself as a lonely man. But Josephine had changed that. Without her in his arms, he felt very lonely. He had to guard against thinking of her when he was riding drag. At night she filled his dreams and not once did the nightmare return.

He never mentioned Josephine or his four months in Benson to the drovers. They would only make fun of him. The only one he could talk to was Whiskey Pete, and Little Blue, of course.

"I had me a good woman once, a fat Injun squaw," Whiskey Pete said. "Ugly as hell, but she sure knew how to take care of me. Taught me to cook too."

"What happened to her?"

"She died birthin'. The baby came out bottom first. Nothin' I could do but watch her die. Baby didn't live either. That's when I give up my own place and started workin' on a ranch. I was drinkin' a lot in them days, goin' most daily to different saloons. I'd step up to the bar, and the tender would say, 'Whiskey, Pete?' And I downed more than a few. The ranch hands thought this was real funny, and whenever they saw me they'd say, 'There goes old Whiskey Pete.' Well, I sobered up and started workin' the chuck wagon, but the name stuck with me."

"Do you mind it?"

"Gawd almighty, no. Just reminds me how much I loved that fat and ugly Injun woman."

"It's a good thing you have Little Blue. He's a mighty fine dog."

"I never had to teach him nothin'. Runnin' the herd comes natural."

Kincade had seen proof of that many times.

Whiskey Pete patted the shaggy head at his feet. "He sure helps with the lonelees."

Kincade reached out to pat Little Blue, but the dog got up and moved to Pete's other side. Kincade laughed. "I'll wait, Little Blue. I understand what it means to care about someone special."

The summer passed at the Sabin ranch. There was always something to do—riding and mending fences, rescuing strays, branding, and such. Whiskey Pete cooked at the ranch house, but he and Kincade would frequently have a second cup of coffee on the porch.

"You met any of the new drovers Sabin has hired for the fall drive?" Whiskey Pete asked one late summer's evening.

"A few."

"Three or four of 'em was talkin' 'bout you."

"Me? Why?"

"Seems one bad hombre named Wil Logan is gunnin' for you. He asked 'em if they knowed which ranch you was at or what herd you'd be drivin'."

"Did they tell him?"

"Hell no. They never knowed you till they signed on here. You better take what they says serious, Kincade."

"The fall drive starts next week. I'll be okay till then."

"Well, watch yer back. These boys say Logan had a real mean look in his eyes."

The fall drive commenced and stretched for days full of endless miles. The closer the drive got to Benson the more Kincade longed for Josephine. He could smell her jasmine perfume in the sage dust, feel her long thighs around his as he rode Digger. The horse's golden mane reminded him of her long silken hair. His dreams drove him crazy as the miles stretched on and on.

But Kincade also grew more fearful for her safety. Around the campfire at night the drovers often recounted the atrocities they had heard about the Logan gang. No mercy was ever shown. Women and girls were violated and then killed. Some were tortured before their husbands' eyes. This must never happen to Josie just because they were lovers.

When he entered Benson he first headed to the bath and barbershop. He wanted to present himself as she liked him best. When he pushed open the batwing doors she rushed into his arms. "Where have you been? You think I didn't know that the herd was here? I've been waiting for an eternity to see you walk through those doors."

He grabbed her and pulled her into a tight embrace. "So I'm here. What are you gonna do about it?"

"Dance, you fool. Dance!"

And they did, with a hunger that seemed never satisfied.

"Josie, I have bad news for you," he said as they lay side by side, finally exhausted. "I've told Sabin, and I've told the boys. Now I must tell you. I can't stay. I'm headed for the far horizons. I don't know where or for how long, but I gotta go."

"No. I want you here. I want you to help me run the Proud Cat. I'll make you my partner."

"Please listen, my love. Logan is after me. He's close. I can smell him. If I stay I'll only endanger you, and that's something I cannot allow to happen. We'll have a few days together, and then I'll get as far away as possible."

She started to cry.

"No tears. Let's make the most of the few days I feel are safe. Maybe someday . . . " and his voice trailed off.

They lay there until the twilight faded. Then they dressed and went to the saloon below. To Kincade's surprise he saw Whiskey Pete and Little Blue.

"My God, look who's here." The two men gave one another rough and hearty hugs.

"Will you have a whiskey, Whiskey Pete?" asked Josie, extending her hand. What with all the stories Kincade had told him about this spectacular woman over the summer, Whiskey Pete felt like he had known Josephine for years. He wrinkled his brow toward Kincade and whispered, "Gawd almighty, pard. You didn't do her justice."

Turning to Josephine, Whiskey Pete replied, "If it's alright with you, ma'am, I'll have what Kincade's havin'. Oh, and if you please, Little Blue likes a saucer of beer now and then— makes him sneeze."

"Finley!" Josephine proudly exclaimed. "Our finest! For the dog!" And the three of them laughed together.

So two tequilas, three beers, and a bowl were brought to the table. They toasted the lady, and then Whiskey Pete said, "Kincade, I heard you was leavin' Sabin and headin' out for the wide open. Me and Little Blue would sure like to come along. How'd you feel about that?"

Kincade thought for a long minute. Why not? "Who's gonna do the cookin'?" he asked with a twinkle in his eye.

"You. I'm tired of my own cookin'. You do cook, don't cha, Kincade?"

11

Kincade, Whiskey Pete, and Little Blue headed out of Benson on a bright, beautiful morning. Kincade was in the lead on Gold Digger, Whiskey Pete followed on his big gray mule Juliet, and Little Blue ran alongside. This would be their parade formation for months. Whiskey Pete was never the leader, he was the follower, and whatever Kincade said or did was okay with him. Kincade chose the trails, the campsites, the time of their bedding down and rising in the morning. If they went into some town's saloon along the way, Kincade would say, "Tequila and a beer chaser." Whiskey Pete would say, "Same as him, and bring a beer for my dog—makes him sneeze."

Unlike Whiskey Pete, Little Blue was a born leader. He found adventure in every mile. He would run far in front, barking for the men to follow. He would scout the terrain on both sides, his black nose sniffing every rock and bush. New smells seemed to invigorate him. His nose just couldn't keep up with all the glorious aromas. Little Blue loved running along riverbanks and then splashing into the water to catch a fish. He would play his old cowdog role, trying to herd the bounding rabbits. About the only time he stayed close to

Kincade and Whiskey Pete was on a very hot day when Little Blue would trot under the mule in the shadow cast by the big animal. Sometimes, Whiskey Pete would put Little Blue on Juliet's rump. The dog could keep his balance even if they galloped.

The three rode in torrential downpours, blistering heat, and unmerciful sandstorms that would almost blind them. But most of their days were sent from heaven. Little Blue began to accept Kincade as the third member of a partnership. He would chase the sticks that Kincade threw. He would stand by the stream as Kincade fished for trout, and he would grab the flopping fish in his mouth as it hit the bank, wagging his tail as if he were doing his part. Kincade would flush out partridges for Little Blue to chase. Kincade loved this playtime with the dog, and Little Blue actually let him rub his head. One night at the campfire Little Blue left Whiskey Pete's side and came to put his head on Kincade's lap.

"Good boy. I knew you'd come my way if I was patient."

Whiskey Pete loved to listen to Kincade tell stories about the places where they were or what they were seeing. They had been riding through junipers, up and into a sage-filled prairie when they found a circle of large stones, mostly grown over.

"You know what this is, Whiskey Pete?"

"Haven't the foggiest. But I bet you're gonna tell me." The men dismounted.

"It's an Indian teepee ring. The Indian would jam a pole into the ground and then put one of these stones as a stopper. Many poles would be placed to make a circle, and all of them would lean toward the center. They'd be tied together at the top, and this was the framework for the buffalo robe cover."

"How come you know all this stuff, Kincade?"

He paused, giving serious thought to Whiskey Pete's question, and decided to reveal a very private part of his life. "I was raised by an old Indian."

"Gawd almighty. You lived in a teepee?"

"Yup. I even had to set it up when we moved around."

"Gawd almighty, ain't you full of surprises."

Realizing that Whiskey Pete hadn't judged him for his upbringing by an old Indian, Kincade pulled the beaded medicine bag from under his shirt. "The old Indian handed this over just before he left me behind. It holds two important secrets."

"You know what they is?"

"Just one." Kincade rolled up his sleeve so Whiskey Pete could see the scarred symbol on his bicep.

"Gawd almighty."

"These first two lines are for my name: Kincade."

"What's the last line?"

"That's one of the missing pieces. I don't know."

"Mind if I take a look at the outside of the bag?" Whiskey Pete asked.

Kincade held it out so Whiskey Pete could see the beaded circle.

"I know what that means," Whiskey Pete proclaimed.

"You do?"

"Yup. Squaw I married had one on the bag she'd made outta elk hide. Those beads stand for the Circle of Life," Whiskey Pete said.

"Go on." It was clear Kincade wanted to understand.

Whiskey Pete scrunched up his forehead, thinking of how to explain the Indian symbol on the face of Kincade's medicine bag. "You know how you meet some folks that's real nice, and then you run into other low-down sidewinders so ornery a cowdog couldn't get along with 'em?"

Kincade listened.

"It's like the two kinds of people balance each other out." Whiskey Pete scratched his head. "It's like a scale to weigh out your gold. Two little pans, one the side of the other. There's a bag 'a dust in one pan, and a different bag in the other. Things balance each other out. That balance is the Circle of Life."

Whiskey Pete continued. "Injuns think everythin' has an opposite that makes a balance—light and dark, rich and poor, strong and weak, full and hungry. You get my meanin'?"

Kincade nodded. "I do."

Pete cleared his throat and pointed to the circle on the bag. "The blue and turquoise are like the sky and the water. That rust color is the earth. The brighter red is for fire. They's opposites that balance. They's the stuff that make up the circle we call life—earth and sky, fire and water. They balance."

Kincade had never paid that much attention to the colors before.

"Then lookee here—the turquoise beads are joined in a line with the red ones. That's cause water and fire is opposites that balance. Do ya get the picture?"

"I do," said Kincade. "Or at least I think I do. So that was the Indian's secret—there are opposite balances that make up a Circle of Life for everybody."

Whiskey Pete nodded. "And all the different colors together around the outside of the circle is because earth and sky, fire and water is what's important to livin'. My squaw was real good at tellin' me that Indian stuff."

"I'm impressed, Whiskey Pete. You've explained the first secret I've wondered about for years. Now see what you can make of the second one—on the inside."

Kincade opened the medicine bag and gave the patch to Whiskey Pete. "One piece of leather, two designs on opposite sides. Does that make a balance?" Kincade asked. Whiskey Pete looked thoughtful. "Maybe." He pointed to one beaded symbol as he returned the leather patch. "That's the same as your arm, Kincade," he said. "That's about all I know," Kincade said with a sigh. He put the bag back in his shirt. Thoughtfully he knelt down, took a palm-sized fist of dirt from the center of the teepee ring, let it run through his fingers and fall back to earth. "I suppose I'll understand it when the time's right."

At the end of a day's ride Whiskey Pete would care for Digger and Juliet. He would loosen their cinch and belly strap, the chest straps, and lower the saddles and bags to the ground. Then off came the blankets. The headstalls were slipped over the ears, releasing the bridles and bits. The animals would lick their chops, glad to be free of the copper. Digger and Juliet never needed to be tied or tethered. They would go about their own business, rummaging for sweet grass.

Kincade would busy himself with the makings of a fire. He would gather sticks, dried sage, and with luck, what was left of a fallen pinion. As the sun began to set, a crackling fire would hold back the darkness. They would eat whatever grub was easy. Then they would talk of the day's events.

Those weeks were the best in Whiskey Pete's life. His heart sang, and he had a spring in his step. When he lay down and pulled the blanket around his shoulders, he would fold his hands behind his head. The sound of Digger and Juliet softly munching the wild grass was so calming, he would be snoring in two minutes.

Kincade would put Digger's saddle blanket under his

bedroll. It wasn't just the padding that was welcome but the smell, which many folks found unpleasant. The musty smell of Digger gave Kincade comfort and peace. With his saddle as a headrest, he would fall asleep almost immediately, hoping for a dream about Josephine.

They had been climbing higher into the hills and bedded down one night on a big flat rock in a meadow of tall grass. When they awoke in the morning they found a lacy, silver fairyland all around them.

"Gawd almighty, ain't that purty," Whiskey Pete said.

"Sure is. I don't remember the Indian name for it, but I call it hoarfrost."

"Frost named for a whore? How about that."

Kincade laughed. "Y'see, all last night spiders the size of little specks wanted to get a look-see at the territory round them. So they slowly inched their way up the stems of the grasses."

"I can just see 'em doin' it," Whiskey Pete said with a grin. He did love Kincade's stories.

"At the top of the stems they looked all around, and then decided it must be better just over there. So, they'd take one or two deep breaths, uncoil a good long string of silk spit, and leap to the top of the next stalk of grass, trailing the string behind them like a fish line."

"Gawd almighty. Ain't that somethin'?"

"When they landed, they'd attach the string to the new piece of grass and start all over again."

"I can see it. Thousands of tiny spiders, all lookin' for somethin' better'n what they got already—right?"

"Yep. Doin' it all night long. Tiny bits of dew got caught on these strings and, as the night got colder, they froze into crystal wires, all glittery and sparkly. That's what you're seeing."

"I like that story, Kincade. But where's the part about the whore?"

Kincade burst out laughing. "Next time I'm tellin' my story to Little Blue. He's got more sense than you."

Kincade thought he knew Whiskey Pete's every mood. He was wrong. Something had begun bothering the big man. Over the next week, Whiskey Pete didn't listen attentively to the stories, he drank his coffee alone, and on the ride he kept Juliet slightly behind Digger. One night around the fire he kicked Little Blue and sent the dog whimpering to Kincade's side. "Okay, Pete. I've had enough. What's put a burr under your saddle?"

Whiskey Pete looked sheepish, then took on a determined frown. He blew air through his lips as if trying to figure out how to say what was on his mind. "It's been a long spell since my squaw died, and I ain't as old as I look. You get my meanin'?"

"You mean it's time to head for a town with a little action?"

"You got my meanin'."

"Do you know how to go to a whore house, Whiskey Pete?"

"So what's there to know? You go in, pay your money, pull down your britches, and go at it."

"No, Whiskey Pete. There's a more proper way—the way of men who know how to Dance."

"I don't want to dance—I just wanna—"

"Just listen, Whiskey Pete, and I'll tell you something that you'll thank me for the rest of your life."

Whiskey Pete called Little Blue back to him and settled down for one of Kincade's stories.

"First, they aren't whores—they're doves. You got that?"

Whiskey Pete nodded. "In town these tempting morsels of flesh will probably be perched gloriously on porches, flaunting their wares, fluttering their fans in front of rouged faces and pouting lips. You got the picture?" Whiskey Pete nodded with an eager grin. "It behooves a cowboy to play his cards smart when riding into this garden of temptation.

"It starts with how you first ride up and address the hitching rail. Pull up smart, back straight, in total and complete command of Juliet, all to make sure the doves are immediately drawn by your arrival. You want every one of those fine and lonely ladies to know that they are in the presence of a real man. You got that?"

"Gawd almighty, I am a real man."

"You stop Juliet, but don't get off. Not yet. Hold for several moments. Then roll your shoulders full circle. Push your chest out, maybe stretching your shirt just a bit, like a rooster who is fluffing up his feathers for the hens in the yard."

Whiskey Pete chortled. "I can do that. I can."

"Following the stretch, jam your cowboy boot into the left stirrup and swing your right leg up high over that cantle of yours, making the sun catch the glint of your silver spurs as you lower your leg slowly to the ground. That makes the jingle-bobs sing."

"Gawd almighty. How'd I ever get along without this lesson?"

"Next Juliet. Do a walk-about, inspecting your mule with conviction and concern. Hold your head still, then nod a bit as if you're pleased at what you see. Then, come up short and take a good look at something as if you're not. No cowboy worth his salt would consider a roll in the hay before first fully attending to his four-legged mount."

Whiskey Pete whooped. "Of course not."

"Now, slide the reins smooth from Juliet's neck, place

them over the rail, not once but twice, to show the doves that Juliet is a fire-breathing beast, barely broke at all."

Whiskey Pete couldn't stop laughing, for no milder mule ever lived than Juliet.

"Finally, and most importantly, step back and look around. Pretend surprise, and then smile as your eyes look at the ladies who've been glued to each and every act of this big, bold, dusty stranger . . . that's you, Whiskey Pete. Gracefully pull off your hat with a wide sweep across your chest, so low that it almost kisses the ground. Swing it back and to the side and gallantly exclaim, 'Ladies!' You do that, and you're gonna see fans fluttering with such speed as to match the beating of their hearts. And that's how to begin the Dance." Kincade folded his hands in his lap.

Whiskey Pete clapped, and Little Blue howled as if he understood every word.

"Great. But you got me scared, Kincade. What if I slip up and forget what comes next? What if they know I'm terrified and quakin' in my boots? What if I catch my spur in the stirrup and sprawl into a pile of what Juliet ate the night before?"

"Then, Whiskey Pete, you just go in, pay your money, pull down your britches, and go at it."

Gypsy was the first town they came to. The outskirts were nothing to brag about, littered with miners' tents, skinny dogs and roosters running this way and that. Chinamen banged on their washboards. Close by were long ropes slung with wet dungarees and union suits that may have once been white but were now a dull gray, especially the drop seats that flapped in the wind. Roofs were canvas, sidewalks dirt paths. Closer to the center of town, the scene improved. Kincade and Pete saw more buckboards, more women with parasols, more businessmen with cigars in their mouths and their thumbs jammed into suspenders, proudly displaying their ample bellies.

About three blocks from the town center there was a double-decked building that sported balconies with ornate railings. Two scantily dressed women leaned against two carved posts. A big sign said THE DOVE NEST.

"There you go, Whiskey Pete," Kincade said. "Get Dancin'!"

"You comin'?"

"And compete with you? No way. I'm gonna find a good saloon. Been awhile since I enjoyed the smell of a good saloon."

The best saloon in Gypsy left something to be desired. But Kincade passed several days playing poker with the money that had been kept at the Proud Cat while he was on the cattle drives. He drank tequila by himself. And he did the Wait, studying those who entered and left. He seldom saw Whiskey Pete. Little Blue came to the saloon a few times, and Kincade would buy the dog a beer. He would lap up a bowl full, sneeze, and then find his way back to where Whiskey Pete hung out. After two weeks, Kincade got restless. He rode Gold Digger to the Dove Nest.

"Hey, Whiskey Pete. Come on out. It's me."

Whiskey Pete emerged, with Little Blue at his heels. "Howdy, Kincade."

"It's time for me to saddle up, pard. You comin'?"

"Didn't know how to tell you before, Kincade, but I think I'll settle down here for awhile. Got me a job as a cook."

Kincade smiled, seeing the dove at Whiskey Pete's back. "Would she be your dessert every night?"

Whiskey Pete blushed. The big man actually blushed.

"Whatever makes you happy, old friend. Little Blue staying with you or riding with me?"

"He likes you, but he don't love you."

"Then I'll be seeing you down the trail. Good luck, Whiskey Pete," and he held out his hand.

"You've been a good pard, Kincade. If you ever need me, you know where to find me."

"I might take you up on that. So long." Kincade tipped his hat to Whiskey Pete's dove, touched his spurs to Digger, and rode out of town.

Ahead lay canyon country for Kincade.

And death.

12

Kincade was surprised at how much he missed—or at least thought about—Whiskey Pete and Little Blue. But he was not given to loneliness except where Josephine was concerned, and he remembered the happy times he had enjoyed with those two buckaroos.

His journey was rambling, with no set direction or goal. The West was spread out from horizon to horizon, like a slowly moving panorama of changes from wilderness to civilization. He could go days seeing only the animals of the desert or forest and birds of the bush or sky. It reminded him of his youth with the old Indian when they would move their camp and he would wonder why.

From time to time he encountered people—people who represented the whole spectrum of Western life. There were homesteaders, ranchers, miners, store operators, and always the saloonkeepers. In the lands that were just opening up, the saloon could be no more than a board put between two sawhorses in a shady spot. A saloon could be a noisy, dirty tent. Sometimes the man who brewed his own poison would sell it off the back of an old wagon. Wherever men gathered to obtain news or swap their stories there would be whiskey for sale.

Kincade longed for the beautiful Proud Cat Dance Hall and Saloon, and even more for its beautiful proprietress.

The West seemed to repeat the same story over and over until suddenly it could astound him with something very unexpected. This was the case when he approached a canyon bottom with a grove of tall cottonwoods where he thought he could find a sheltered campsite.

There in the middle next to a stream sat an abandoned two-story house. It must have been a fine place in its day. The entire first story was surrounded by a wide and generous porch.

Kincade rode up to the front and tied Gold Digger to the rail. He swung off and stepped onto the deck. Testing each step on the rotting wood, Kincade turned back to survey the land. He could see the remnants of a corral that was fenced on three sides with the canyon's cliff face as its fourth side. To the left, a narrow canyon wound upward so a rider could move to the canyon rim without too much difficulty.

He turned back to the house and peeked through shattered glass windows into a great room. It looked like a saloon dance hall. Moving eight feet to his right, Kincade pushed open a creaking front door and stepped inside. It *was* a dance hall, or in more proper terms, a ballroom.

To the left rear sat a raised platform. Surrounding it, hardwood floorboards showed considerable use. How odd, Kincade thought, that this place would be found in the middle of the Apache lands.

Almost unconsiously, Kincade fingered the old medicine bag beneath his shirt. He pulled it out and looked at the Circle of Life as Whiskey Pete had explained it to him. Maybe it was true with this old house. A white man must have made a stab at this place, this very remote piece of untamed frontier. This must have been some sort of meeting place. Kincade tried to imagine courageous settlers gathering their families, traveling for great distances, all to mingle, laugh, and share precious moments amid all this loneliness and danger. There must have been some fine times within these walls. Kincade closed his eyes and tried to hear the ghosts of fiddles and clapping hands. This house showed evidence of wealth, of pride, of friendship.

But on the other side of the Circle of Life, Kincade could imagine failure, shame, and loneliness. The abandonment of such a fine dwelling must have given someone great heartache. Did a wife long for her friends and family back East, even though her husband tried to build a similar lifestyle for her here? Or did a husband die and leave his wife no alternative but to forsake what they had built together? Was he a rancher who lost his herd to the Apache? Was she an invalid who had an addiction to laudanum, as so many women did? Or was this white man a lonely bachelor who returned East to find a bride?

In this pensive mood, Kincade opened the drawstring of the pouch and took out the scrap of leather with designs on each side. "Where is my counterbalance?" he asked himself. "The joy of loving Josephine, and the pain of being without her? That I understand, but it's not the answer to this mystery. The old Indian made this for me, and he never knew Josephine. There is some answer right here if I could only solve it."

Kincade put the leather back and slipped the medicine bag inside his shirt. Suddenly and without warning, Gold Digger screamed. Kincade instinctively twisted, putting his hands on his twin Colts, moving swiftly to the open front door.

Whatever the thing was that spooked Gold Digger, it was fast. The hair stood up on its head, its feet scurrying like gusts of wind kicking up dust. Gold Digger's reins pulled tight from the hitching rail, as the stallion strained to break free. As Kincade blew through the doors, he yanked both Colts from the holsters, cocking twin hammers in the process.

Within seconds, Kincade rocked back and laughed. "Digger, that's just a whistle pig."

Gold Digger's master pointed to the now scurrying ball of fur. "'Bout the biggest rodent you've ever seen, isn't he?" He laughed again, as the raccoon-sized woodchuck scuttled around the corner of the house. Kincade felt good as days of tension yielded to the simple and unbridled pleasure releasing inside his chest. It had been too long since he had laughed, far too long.

Gold Digger didn't think it was funny.

"Okay, okay, I know you were startled, fella," soothed Kincade. "I must have spooked him when the floorboards creaked. Just think how scared he must have been seeing something the size of you."

The stallion took stock of himself, shook his golden mane, flexed his considerable chest muscles once or twice, and otherwise gathered his pride. Once done, he looked over at Kincade with as much aloofness as a palomino could muster.

"You know, Digger," Kincade smiled, "this shows that even you are a part of the Circle of Life. When we're riding drag, you've got the courage of a hero. But just now you were as timid as a schoolgirl seeing a mouse. It's like Whiskey Pete says, 'Things balance each other out.'"

Digger didn't think this incident was the slightest bit funny.

Kincade stepped from the planks and onto the ground. "What do you think, Digger?"

The horse responded by tugging at his reins, letting his master know that he would just as soon be up out of this canyon where he, and Kincade, could get a good look around, and not be surprised by whistle pigs and such, whatever a whistle pig was.

Kincade untied Gold Digger, swung into the saddle, and gave the reins a flick. "Come on, Digger. This place makes me think too much." They headed up the arroyo to the canyon rim above.

Days followed days of barren prairie scattered with clumps of sage and mesquite, of bleached earth where grasses struggled for life . . . miles and miles of vast high desert, lanced with mountains and ripped open by streams. The sun traveled its journey from the forbidding chill of black night to the zenith of the scorching noonday, and back into ink again. Stars and moon might be seen or hidden. The wind blew north to south, sometimes west to east. The sameness made Kincade feel that he *was* the scene and not just passing through it.

When he thought of Josephine it was with such longing that tears filled his eyes. And yet he was on this strange migration to protect her—to keep her free from the vengeance of Wil Logan. How long could he continue? He never calculated the future, only the passing of one day at a time.

Gold Digger smelled it first. His nostrils flared, and his ears went forward as if a sound might be in the wind also. There was something unfamiliar burning. Sage was a part of the odor, but that wasn't it alone. Kincade and the stallion headed straight into the smell.

They came to a rise. Below them ran a clear creek and the gulch that held it. Just beyond a clump of riverbank cottonwoods stood a humble sod hut, smoke wafting up from a hole in the roof. Now Kincade recognized the smell from his days with the old Indian. It wasn't from wood, as there was little of that here. This fire was fueled by dried buffalo dung.

Gold Digger strode down the bank toward the soddy. Kincade never took a situation like this one lightly. His deep blue eyes darted left, then right—near, then far—scanning the ridge ahead and behind, looking first up and then down the arroyo where the soddy stood. This was, after all, the land of the Mescalero Apache.

Chickens pecked and scratched around the yard supervised by a protective rooster, and a crude wire pen held two thin sheep and a single black and white cow. Kincade swung from the saddle, leaving his palomino to drink at the stream. "Hello the cabin," he called. As he did so, a thin woman stepped from the doorway. A white woman.

Her auburn hair was tied to the top of her head in a knot. When worn down, it must have been long. But for the moment, she would have none of that. She was at her business, apron affixed, flour covering both hands, squinting into the late morning sun and the face of Kincade.

"Mornin'," offered Kincade, touching his hat.

"I don't believe I've seen another person, other than him, for what seems like a lifetime now," said the woman, who couldn't have been much older than twenty. "You know where you are, mister?"

"I do."

"Then you must be a fool," said the woman.

"Some have said as much," answered Kincade.

The woman waited, standing silently, slowly brushing the flour from her hands. "You look hungry," she said.

"I am."

"I'm baking bread," she said, cautiously warming to the

stranger who apparently meant her no harm. "Would you like some?"

"I would, ma'am."

"I ain't got no butter, but there's wild berry jam that was here a'ready. I couldn't take nothin' from the wagon." At her mention of the word "wagon," Kincade could see the woman's brow suddenly tighten. Something bad flashed very briefly, something in her eyes.

"That would be heaven sent," smiled Kincade.

She smiled, slightly. "This ain't heaven, stranger, but the bread is fresh."

With that, Kincade opened a wire fence gate and stepped into the yard. The woman disappeared into the black opening of the only door, reappearing after several minutes with a tattered remnant of white linen that held a slice of still steaming bread, topped with jam.

She walked up to Kincade and held out her hands to him.

"I do thank you," said Kincade, taking a bite. "I've been riding for some time now."

"You look it."

"I feel it."

The woman tried to smile again. "Where would you be goin', stranger?"

"Name's Kincade."

"Kincade what?"

"That's it. Just Kincade. Never had a last name that I know of. I'm headed north."

"What for?"

Kincade didn't answer as he took another bite. His deep blue eyes looked straight into hers.

"Well, I guess that's your business and none 'a mine," she replied. "Though I'd be careful if I was you. The Apache don't cotton to white men. You'd best move on."

"How is it you're here?" asked Kincade.

Her head jerked, but for only a moment. "Him," she answered. "He's Apache." From behind the soddy a limb snapped, and the woman jumped, holding her hands over her head, as though something hard was about to strike her. It was only the cow stepping on a fallen branch.

Kincade looked at her white skin. She was young. "Oh." He searched her eyes.

"He's been out huntin' for meat since before sunrise," she continued. "He'll be back anytime now. You better go."

Kincade finished the last bite, handing the linen back to the woman and licking the last of the jam off his fingers. He wondered how on earth she had ended up here, with an Apache, in the middle of nowhere. He asked no further questions.

"Thank you for your hospitality, ma'am," he said.

She nodded, looking into Kincade's eyes. Something was there . . . a deep fear. He could see it in her eyes. Something she wanted to say. But she wouldn't. Maybe she couldn't.

Kincade turned on his heel, walked back through the wire gate, took Digger's reins, swung up, and waited.

"Thanks again, ma'am."

"It's not 'ma'am.' My name's Cissy—Cissy Dye."

Kincade turned Gold Digger away from the stream, up the bank to the north, topped the rim, stopped, and looked back. She stood as he had left her, hands frozen at her sides, absolutely still.

Her terror forbade her to cry out, to beg the stranger to save her life from the Apache she referred to as "him." The former nineteen-year-old wife and mother of the Dye family knew that if she breathed a word about the attack and slaughter of her entire family as their wagon moved across the plains of Wyoming after leaving Julesburg an eon ago, if she said one word, Cissy Dye knew that her Apache keeper would not only take her scalp, but sever the head of the man who now looked at her from the top of the gulch . . . a man who had just eaten a freshly baked sliver of simple bread . . . a man with no last name.

She strained her eyes to see the top of the hillside. He waved at her and then rode north and out of sight. She knew she had lost her only chance to tell someone of the horror in which she now lived and breathed.

Tears silently coursed down the face of Cissy Dye, the sole survivor of the Dye family.

13

In the upper reaches of the Dry Head Canyon there were clear water springs bubbling from deep within the earth. As they flowed south, more and more tributaries joined the first, until a creek had become a stream, the stream a river. A river with considerable force.

It was plain how the canyon had become so deep, the side walls so steep. Since the beginning of time, the water had continued to rip an ever-deepening gash into the rock and dirt, tearing and taking the soil and stone with it. Now more than a half-mile wide, and nearly as deep, the Dry Head was a formidable sight to be seen. It was named for the bones and bleached skulls that littered the canyon floor, remnants of thousands upon thousands of buffalo.

When the Indians were first introduced to the Spanish horses, the world began to change for the buffalo. Later, the Henry repeating rifle blew a cold wind across the land. It gave its shooter the ability to load and fire fifteen cartridges as quickly as he wished, leading to the slaughter of millions of buffalo. But after the horse, and before the rifle, there was Dry Head Canyon.

The skilled Apache hunters would gather on their painted

war ponies so the buffalo herd was between them and the Dry Head Canyon. Then, bursting over the grassy ridges, the proud and resourceful Apaches would whoop and holler, racing like the wind toward the herd. As they had done for centuries, the herd would bolt, knowing it could outrun, or certainly outlast, the Apache.

But they couldn't outwit or outrun the Dry Head Canyon.

Thundering buffalo hooves led to hysteria within the stampeding herd. Their only thought was escape from the onslaught of arrows. Run they would, with great speed, followed by hundreds of others running just as fast at their heels, all chased by the warriors on horseback.

The Apache were smart. They weren't chasing. They were guiding the beasts straight toward the rim of the Dry Head.

The leaders of the buffalo herd would reach the edge first, jamming their hooves deep in a desperate attempt to stop before sailing off the edge and into the deep abyss below. It would have worked, if it hadn't been for the hundreds of others just behind, all stampeding forward, ramming into the leaders in mass, and launching them over the lip.

Once the second wave of bison struck, the same fate fell to the third bunch, which was then rammed by the fourth wave of the panicked herd. Consequently, the bottom of the Dry Head was a graveyard. Thousands of bleached bones over thousands of years. Tens of thousands of skulls . . . of dry heads.

The Apache were wise hunters. They knew just how long to press their attack so as to not deplete the herd. They needed just enough meat and hide to serve the tribe. No more. The buffalo was their lifeblood, and they owed their lives to the beasts. Without them they would die.

Kincade and Gold Digger slowly wound their way up the

canyon floor, surveying the remnants of generations of buffalo, of generations of the hunted. The air was perfectly quiet, and still. "Easy, fella," soothed Kincade. "Their time is over."

Little did either of them know they were headed toward a killing machine.

High on the rim stood a paint horse. A red-skinned man, with jet-black hair fanned over his head, naked but for a breechcloth, straddled it bareback. A full quiver of arrows hung over his shoulder. At his waist hung a razor-sharp tomahawk.

Kincade and Gold Digger were headed straight toward a vengeful Apache who prided himself on the number of white men he had scalped and the one white woman he had kept for himself. This was one of the renegades who had shot flaming arrows into the canvas of five wagons headed for California. His own arrows had pierced the terrified children of the Dye family and their grandmother who tried to shield them. He had ridden off with the young mother while others set fire to the wagons.

He had never mated with a white woman. What would her naked body look like? Would she fight him off or succumb to his powerful masculinity? If she pleased him he would keep her—if not, he would kill her and display her scalp.

The Indian had been tracking and watching the white man who rode the magnificent horse. He had never seen such an animal. Its golden hide was so unlike the brown and white paint ponies of the Apache. The tail and mane were the same honey color, long and full, waving in the wind. He would have this horse for his own, and he would take pleasure in killing the man who rode it.

For three days he had learned this man's habits, how he

moved, how he slept, judging his skills just as a mountain lion would watch a lost sheep.

The hunter had learned all he needed. He began his first move toward his unsuspecting prey . . .

14

Shadows came early to the Dry Head. So would that night's camp.

As Kincade and Gold Digger rode up a draw toward the rim of the Dry Head Canyon, the Apache moved quietly. The Indian's footsteps were like whispers on the wind. Not a sound. The quiver and bow were left behind. This white man would be taken by tomahawk, his scalp hung over the door of the Apache's soddy where his white woman would be reminded of the superiority of red men.

The top of the arroyo fanned out onto a vast plain. The wind whipped this open range, stripping it of all vegetation higher than a few inches. This windblown plateau was no place to camp. But closer to the canyon rim, Kincade could see the juniper had taken hold, providing shelter. Kincade and the stallion pulled to the right, and back toward the lip of the canyon where he planned to set up camp for the night.

The Apache had wisely left his paint horse downwind from Kincade's palomino. The white man would be easy prey. But there was something about the palomino that gave the Apache pause, something more than his golden horseflesh, his nearly blond mane and long tail. It was something about the way his ears would quickly twitch this way and that. There was something about the stallion's eyes, always watching. He would make that beast forget the white man. He would show it who was master even if he had to whip it.

The junipers would do a fine job protecting Kincade and Gold Digger from the ceaseless winds. They would also have ample firewood that evening, all nearly within arm's reach. The days may have been blistering, but the darkness brought freezing cold. A fire would be a godsend tonight.

Kincade rode close to the canyon rim, making sure he had a good look-see on anything approaching from below. The view would also be a real pleasure. Tomorrow morning would be a spectacular sight, watching the dawn's sun pull back the deep shadows on the canyon walls.

From the mannerisms of the Apache and Kincade they might have been blood brothers. They were each keen watchers. They moved cautiously. They each knew the benefit of being patient before making their move. They each had seen their share of the unforgiving face of danger, and each had survived. Both men shared the ways and the skills of the Native American.

But only one of them would leave the canyon rim alive.

Gold Digger didn't need to be picketed. All Kincade needed to do was slip off the slick-fork saddle, gently remove the Salinas Port bit from his teeth, and Digger would go about his own business while Kincade went about his. The stallion was soon free of tack, rummaging amid the junipers, looking for sweet grass.

Kincade busied himself with the makings of fire. He would make camp on the edge of the rim, where the smoke would be carried over the canyon, and down, making for a clear evening, and a good dispersal of smoke along the canyon floor, assuring him of not sending up an open invitation to any renegade Indians that he and his horse were there for the picking.

The Apache watched. His brow furrowed just a bit as he looked at Kincade. The white men usually built big fires and stood back from the flame. But this one built a small fire and stayed close. Smart, he thought, and too bad. A big fire would have thrown greater light, which might have helped this white man see the face of death when the Indian made this camp his killing field.

It didn't matter to the Apache. He would soon have the white man's horse and his scalp as well. The Apache's brow smoothed at the thought, and a very slight hint of a smile appeared for a fleeting moment.

Kincade laid Gold Digger's saddle blanket on the ground and then stretched his bedroll on top. He would be comforted again by the musty smell of horse, usually distasteful to most people. He set his saddle at one end for a headrest. He smiled inwardly with a sense of satisfaction.

Once done, Kincade pulled a chunk of jerky from the saddlebag. As he did so, his mind wandered to the thin white woman, of the pain in her eyes and the silence on her lips.

The Apache was behind Kincade now, only two hundred feet away. Patience . . .

A sadness flooded back to Kincade for the white woman, made even whiter by the crippling fear of the male she referred to as "him." How had she ever come to be in that mud house? What had happened to the family who must have once cherished her? He suddenly felt he had to do something for this woman. He had to help lessen the pain she felt. Why hadn't she said anything? Kincade bit into the jerky with a tight jaw. The peace he had felt at the fireside vanished.

Quietly. Slowly. The Indian was good as his craft. Years of sneaking up on prey had taught him well.

Now a hundred feet away.

There's nothing I can do for her tonight, thought Kincade. But in the morning, I'll turn back.

To shake the tenseness from his muscles, Kincade stepped away from the fire and moved to the rim. The view from the edge would give him peace, at least for this night. Yes, the view from the very edge, looking into the half-mile abyss below, would give him peace.

The Apache's grip on the tomahawk tightened. Now seventy-five feet away. The white man's back was all he could see. A nice target. He would split that spine in two, and then the horse would be his. No fighting. It was going to be easy.

Kincade could see how this gorge had come to be such an effective tool for gathering meat over the centuries. The canyon walls were so sheer, so vertical, one step off the rim and the buffalo would suffer a half-mile free fall, smashing into the rocks at the base, immediately killed upon impact.

Not a sound as the Apache approached. Not a crack of a twig, not a rustle of a leaf. Nothing. Absolutely quiet. Fifty feet.

Kincade began to feel the tenseness leave his arms. His fists began to unclench. The lines in his forehead began to unknot. Tomorrow, Kincade. Yes, you'll help her tomorrow, he thought to himself. Relax . . .

Kincade reached down to the silver and gold buckles on his gunbelts, releasing and removing the weapons from his waist. There, that feels better, he thought. He lowered his pistols to the ground.

Too easy. This was all too easy. The Apache silently moved his right hand holding the razor-sharp tomahawk, perfectly balanced for throwing, up and back of his right shoulder. As it had countless times, the blade would fly like the wind, hitting the target within an instant, splitting it in half. Or at the very least, burying itself to the shaft as it tore into the flesh. Twenty-five feet. Ripping this white man in two was simply too easy. The Indian paused. I'll feel no pleasure if I open this white man's skull without first seeing the fear in his eyes, thought the Indian. I must not throw this weapon, but sink it with my own thrust. Then I will see his eyes fill with terror. His fear . . . that is what will bring me pleasure when I crack his skull.

I must touch him first . . .

So the Apache lowered his tomahawk and crept the last hushed footsteps remaining between him and this white man. The white man with the magnificent horse that would soon be his.

Kincade breathed deeply, looking down into the canyon, looking downward over one-half mile to the floor below, savoring the aroma of the junipers to his left and right. He could not yet smell the living horror approaching him from behind.

Less than fifteen feet to go . . .

It all happened so fast.

One moment, a vast and silent peace, a spectacular vista, kissed by graceful winds, a place were a man could take stock of his life, where he had been, what might lay ahead, and what this Circle of Life meant.

In the next instant, Kincade felt like his ears had been cracked open like an egg and filled with the loud warning shout of a terrified voice. It was a woman's voice. A voice he knew.

Her scream was so startling, so vivid, Kincade snapped back to reality and found his body twisting fast, dropping like a stone to the ground. It was an instinctive reflex motion, lightning quick.

Halfway around, Kincade stared into the wild eyes of the Apache and glimpsed the cutting edge of a well-used tomahawk, gleaming in the last rays of a setting sun, slashing downward with blurring speed, slicing the air exactly where the back of Kincade's skull had been only a split second earlier.

Had the woman not screamed a blink of an eye earlier, Kincade's skull would have been shattered by the redskinned banshee towering above him. She had saved his life.

Within another heartbeat, the Apache realized that somehow, the white man had been alerted, and reacted with such speed that the Indian had been taken completely by surprise. He had been so careful, so quiet in his approach. He had been so good at this game of death for so many years. What happened? This couldn't be!

Kincade's back slammed into the red rock lip of the canyon's outermost rim. As his left shoulder blade struck the ground, the muscles in his gut contracted to twist his body in a rolling motion. But a twist to the south would send Kincade spinning over the edge, and into the void. A twist to the north would send him squarely into the legs of the Apache, whose tomahawk was now arching up and over his head, gathering even more speed at its zenith, accelerating to deliver a tremendous blow to the cowboy now trapped at his feet.

Almost at the same instant as the warning scream came a shrill whistle, followed by an unearthly screech.

Could it be from her? No, this shriek was not a human utterance, but the primeval outcry of a predator. It electrified the air just as the Apache prepared to make his kill.

He never knew what hit him until it was too late . . .

15

What happened was so surreal, so unexpected, so unexplainable that the very thought of it approached the supernatural.

As the Apache's tomahawk began its downward arch, an earsplitting screech filled the canyon, echoing off its walls. Both men looked up. The shriek came from an enormous shadow, moving incredibly fast, dropping from the heavens. Except this shadow had substance, coupled with a killing power that far exceeded the Apache's.

Before Kincade's astonished eyes, and with breathtaking swiftness, a huge eagle slammed squarely into the face of the Apache.

Its talons extended into slashing knives, burying themselves into the wide eyes of the Indian. The gelatinous orbs exploded like ripe grapes, spraying blood over both men. The blinded Apache screamed and dropped the tomahawk, clawing at his mutilated face.

At the same instant that the winged shadow swooped from the sky, Kincade heard the pounding gallop of his golden palomino. He snatched up the tomahawk and somersaulted back, just in time to avoid the crushing hooves of Gold Digger.

Without hesitation and at a full gait, Gold Digger's massive chest crashed squarely into the back of the writhing Indian with the force of a runaway train. Just before the moment of the stallion's impact, the eagle withdrew its claws, lifting its wings up and back, as though it were parting a curtain to make way for the charging horse.

Gold Digger's collision lifted the Indian six feet into the air. The breath was pounded from his lungs, his hands flailed the air. A guttural scream left his lips as the red man sailed out, over, and into the Dry Head Canyon. Then, the Apache felt the same horror as the tens of thousands of buffalo who had met the same fate over a millennium, except that the buffalo had been able to see the canyon floor rush up to meet them. The Indian could not.

It was just as well. For squarely beneath the cliff, one-half mile below the canyon rim, sat an ancient stone the size of a house. When it first fell from the canyon's wall eons ago, the collision with the valley floor had exploded the rock, cleaving it in half, exposing a midsection core of solid granite that refused to shatter, turning it into an indestructible stone spire. At a tremendous speed, the Apache's body smashed into the eighteen-foot-tall granite spike. The Indian's torso exploded, spitting bone fragments, bits of flesh, and shattered spine into the air.

It was over within a matter of seconds.

The canyon fell silent. Gold Digger stood protectively over his master, chest calming, pulse slowing. The eagle lifted higher and higher, in a spiraling thermal. Kincade began to rise from his backside, shaking to clear his head. He watched the eagle as it leveled off, paused, and then begin a slow descent as though it were returning to a nest on the canyon's rim. Kincade rubbed his eyes in utter disbelief. It wasn't a nest to which the eagle was returning. It was to the extended right arm of a human being, obviously its master, its handler.

There, standing before Kincade, was the thin white woman who had offered him a slice of freshly made bread. She no longer had fear in her eyes. The finality of what had just happened to the Indian had brought her an inner strength that had been robbed from her, by "him." Stolen since the day the Apache had attacked the Dye family wagon, when she had been forced to watch the slaughter of her entire family. Robbed from her as she had been gagged and bound over the Apache's paint horse, taken to a godforsaken mud hut hellhole, terrified into doing his bidding, into being his squaw.

But the tables had turned in a way no human being could have ever imagined.

Three months earlier, the Indian had left her alone for more than seven weeks, knowing she couldn't escape, as there was no place for her to run. And even if she had tried, Cissy Dye knew he would track her down and skin her alive. On the third morning of being alone, she found the eagle by the creek, wounded. The moment the bird saw her, it tried to unfurl its wings, but couldn't. She stayed perfectly still, thirty feet away, in order not to alarm the eagle. After an hour, she knelt down, the eagle's eyes locked onto hers. At sunset, she slowly stood, and ever so carefully walked to within ten feet of the huge bird. Dusk turned into night, and the night into dawn. She waited, not moving, as the eagle began to understand this human being meant it no harm.

On the afternoon of that second day, Cissy offered the eagle a piece of dried jerky, taken from the torn pocket of her apron. Moving slowly, to within three feet, she reached out and silently placed the meat within its reach, withdrawing her hand and herself to a distance of five feet.

For the next hour, the eagle watched her, not moving. Then, it took the meat. Cissy took another piece of jerky from her apron. The two ate together.

She spent her second night near the bird, still, hardly moving. Cissy Dye was so determined, so focused on her escape from the Apache, that a wild idea consumed her. She had always been good with animals. Though she had never had contact with anything like the magnificent winged creature now a few feet from her, she knew, and could see, just how dangerous the predator was. Its claws were ferocious, the hooked beak created to rip flesh from bone. Its golden eyes stared at her from a bottomless depth.

The morning of the third day, Cissy decided to make her move. She edged to within a foot of the raptor. Wrapping her apron round and round her right arm, she placed it before, and then under, the eagle's claws, gently rolling the fabric up and under, up and under, until finally the bird grabbed the cloth.

With her free hand, she tore a piece of petticoat, cupped it, and softly placed it over the eagle's head. It took all her strength to lift the bird. It was heavier than she had expected, strong, much stronger than she imagined. And powerful.

Cissy had found a fallen cottonwood. She had broken up and arranged branches, fashioning a crude nest. Now she walked up the arroyo, holding the eagle still as it gripped her right forearm. Kneeling, she laid the eagle into this wooden cradle, removed the cloth hood, and placed another piece of jerky next to its head.

The bird looked at it, looked at her, and ate.

For the next six weeks, she cared for the injured raptor, replacing the jerky with the livers of slaughtered rabbits. By an amazing and time-consuming sequence of events, the bird began to trust her. As its wing healed, rather than fly the bird would wait for her to return to the nest. Her approach was always cautious, respectful, always caring, never alarming. Her voice soothing, her hands gentle.

The woman began to encourage the bird to take wing, gently lifting him, thrusting her right arm skyward, protecting her flesh from the razor-sharp claws as the eagle would flap its wings, gathering air. She would have to rock her head to the side when the bird lifted off, as its wingspan was wider than she was tall.

The eagle fully recovered and regained its mastery of the sky. But it would always return to her, no matter how high, no matter how far, it flew. She and this glorious bird had bonded. They had become of one mind. And the one mind knew that the Apache was destined, at their hands, to one day be torn apart.

Cissy fashioned a crude scarecrow, attempting to make it look as much like the Apache as possible. In the eye sockets of its face, she placed two bits of rabbit liver. Returning to the bird, lifting it with her shielded arm, she would shrill and whistle, releasing the creature, who would climb, hover, and then swoop down to the scarecrow to retrieve its entrails reward.

Over and over and over, Cissy Dye and the enormous eagle practiced the attack and reward on the Apache scarecrow. Their practice had perfect results. The proof was now at the bottom of Dry Head Canyon.

16

Kincade stood with his back to the canyon, stunned, looking at the very young widow Cissy Dye. At the mud hut, she
had looked so fragile, so weak. But now, with the eagle
perched on her right arm, she and the bird were the most
unearthly and formidable display of raw power that he could
ever remember seeing. Woman and beast looked at
Kincade, unblinking.

The woman began to move forward, toward Kincade,
almost like a specter. Slowly, but with steeled determination,
she walked past Kincade, moving to the edge of the rim. She
looked down, far down, at the shattered corpse of the
Apache. She didn't move. Neither did Kincade.

After a few moments, she raised her head, looked across
the canyon and to what lay beyond. Kincade could see her
shoulder blades arch slightly back, up, around, down and
back again. She was removing a terrible pain from deep
within her body. He recognized the ritual. He had used it
himself.

Then, as Kincade watched, she turned to the eagle, whose
golden catlike eyes stared back into hers. She leaned forward, bringing her lips to nearly touch the feathers on its

head. She whispered something that Kincade could not make out and then moved her head back.

The eagle looked deeply into the eyes of the woman who had saved his life. His eyes blinked. Once.

Then, with a movement that reminded Kincade of water gliding over smooth river rock, the eagle unfurled his massive wings, and like a wave, sent them downward, upward, and down once again, lifting off the arm of a nineteen-year-old girl. The raptor climbed, caught an updraft from the canyon floor, soared, caught another, circled, higher still, rising toward the sun. Gradually, the bird disappeared from sight.

She turned to face Kincade. For the first time since Kincade had been nearly hacked to pieces, Cissy Dye spoke. "I guess his horse is mine now."

Kincade walked into the junipers where the Apache's paint waited. He took the reins of the rope bridle and brought the Indian's horse over to the woman. "You going back to the soddy?"

"Nothin' there I want. The only person I ever loved was lost near a place in northeastern Colorado. They call it Julesburg. I hope to find my little girl's grave there. Help me up."

Kincade knelt down, enabling the young woman to step on his back and boost herself onto the woven blanket that covered the horse's spine. He handed her the reins.

Walking over to Gold Digger, Kincade removed the oiled duster from the saddle skirt, walked back to the woman, and passed it up to her. He reached into his pocket, gathered several gold coins, and placed them in her small hand.

"Thank you, Kincade."

"I better ride with you."

"No. I've learned to take care of myself." She looked into

Kincade's eyes, and he saw undeniable power within hers. Considering everything this young woman had suffered, all that she had lost, and what he had just witnessed on the rim of the Dry Head Canyon, he sensed Cissy was a very unusual woman.

"Good-bye and good luck, Cissy Dye."

She reined left, nudged the pinto, and rode away. Kincade could only watch as she finally disappeared into the sage and scrub. Why, he wondered, had this woman ever been put in this horrible situation? Where were the men in her life when she needed them most? Why hadn't they been at her side, protecting her?

Suddenly, the realization hit Kincade like a cracked whip. Leaving Josephine in Benson, alone, unprotected, had been a terrible mistake. Wil Logan was sure to find, torture, and kill her just to have vengeance on his childhood enemy. Kincade should have stayed by her side. He should have never left her!

Kincade gathered his tack, saddled and leaped onto Gold Digger, leaning into the stallion's neck as his spurs jammed into the palomino's ribs. The horse reared and launched into a full gallop.

He should have stayed with Josephine!

17

The days and nights Kincade spent racing to Benson were a lurid nightmare. The ghostlike stare from Cissy Dye's vacant eyes haunted him. The pain she had suffered tortured Kincade as he imagined the peril in which he had placed Josephine. What could he have possibly been thinking? Logan knew from their childhood together that attacking anything or anyone Kincade cared about was as brutally effective as bludgeoning Kincade himself. If Logan grabbed Josephine, he would have Kincade at his mercy.

"I should have never left her!"

Five agonizing days after Kincade left the Dry Head Canyon, a thoroughly exhausted Gold Digger approached the outskirts of Benson. But Kincade knew immediately that something was wrong. He smelled it before he actually saw it.

There, at the center of Benson, lay the very cold remains of the Proud Cat Dance Hall and Saloon. It had been burned to the ground. Only the charred ruins of a few walls stood like black ghosts in a cemetery of gray ashes.

Kincade grabbed the first person who passed by. "My God, man. What happened here?"

"Proud Cat got set afire about a month back."

"Miss Josephine? What about her?"

"Mr. Finley got Miss Josie, and they ran outside. She just had on her nightdress, but he helped her jump on her black horse, and she took off in the dark."

"Then she's safe." Kincade breathed a sigh of relief. "Do you know who set the fire?"

"Mr. Finley recognized 'em. It was a gang of five outlaws, led by a huge ugly man. They set the place on fire. The flames and smoke was everywhere. You could barely see.

"The biggest outlaw kept yellin', 'Kincade, you in there? Kincade!' That was when Finley recognized him: Wil Logan."

Kincade knew it. "Did Finley see his face on the wanted posters?"

"No. This Logan fella was the killer who murdered Finley's wife and boy. He's the same fella burned Josie's station on the Cherokee."

"Oh God." Kincade couldn't believe what he was hearing.

"Logan's gang grabbed Mr. Finley, took their six-shooters and blew off both his knees. Then, they threw him back into the flames. Whole building was goin' up. Logan was laughin' like he was crazy. Said, 'Tell yer wife and kid you'll see 'em in hell!' Mr. Finley, he got burned up."

Kincade was out of his mind in rage.

"Logan and his gang got back on their horses. They was ridin' back and forth in front of ever'body. They shot two fellas who was tryin' to throw water on the fire. He yelled at ever'body, 'I'm Wil Logan. Tell Kincade it was me. Logan, you understand?' Then they galloped off. Nobody here dared follow 'em."

Kincade clenched his fists. "Do you know where Josephine went?"

"There's rumor she's in Tombstone. But I don't know for sure."

"Tombstone? Why there?"

"She knew a fella owned a big hotel on Allen Street. Place called the Cosmopolitan. He's real rich. Been tryin' to get Josephine to leave the Proud Cat for a long time, open up a new saloon in the Cosmopolitan. Finley said the fella offered to give her half ownership. Knew he'd make a lot 'a money off her if she'd do it. But she kept sayin' no." The man looked at the ruins of the Proud Cat. "Logan changed all that. Rumor has it she's in Tombstone. But I don't know for sure."

Kincade galloped out of town with guilt following him like a shadow. "I should have stayed to protect her from Logan. Instead I rode away hoping he wouldn't reach her. Or was I just a coward? Now look what's happened. The Proud Cat gone, Finley dead, Josephine on the run. Oh God. Why didn't I stay in Benson? Well, I'm gonna make up for it now."

He put his spurs to Digger and ate up the miles he had just covered. "I'll pick up Whiskey Pete in Gypsy just in case there's trouble in Tombstone. I can count on him." He rode day and night with only brief stops to let Gold Digger rest. Sleep was impossible for him.

It was early, and there were no girls on the porch when Kincade pulled up in front of the Dove Nest and jumped down from his saddle. He bounded up the steps and banged on the door. In a moment a yawning, tousled girl opened the door.

"Where's Whiskey Pete? Get him. It's important."

"You new in town, mister?"

"What difference does that make? Call Whiskey Pete."

"He ain't here, mister. Whiskey Pete's dead."

"He's what?"

"Oh yes. He's very much dead. Me and the girls bought his coffin and laid him in the cemetery a couple 'a weeks ago. Had him a nice grave marker too."

Kincade was in the middle of a living hell. "How'd he die?"

"Outlaws—that's how. In the middle of the night five of 'em yanked him out of bed. Didn't even let him put his britches on before they dragged him away. His dog Little Blue followed 'em, barkin' and nippin' at their horses' legs. They had a camp outside town with a hot fire. Four of 'em tied Whiskey Pete to a tree. Then some fella . . . name 'a Logan . . . got right up inta Whiskey Pete's face. He was yellin', 'Where's Kincade? I know you was ridin' with him. You know where he is. Better tell us if you know what's good for you.' But Whiskey Pete wouldn't say nothin'. He spit in Logan's face."

Kincade felt dizzy, gulping air to steady himself. "How do you know all this?"

"The boy that sweeps our floors heard the racket—the dog barkin' 'n all. He followed, but not too close. He hid in the trees. He was damn lucky not to get caught."

"How did Whiskey Pete die?"

"Well, you know that dog of his, Little Blue? The leader—you know, that Logan fella—hit the dog over the head with the butt of his shotgun. Then his boys skinned Little Blue and put him on a spit. Roasted him over their fire like he was a pig right in front of Whiskey Pete, who was cryin' like a baby."

"No! No! God, no!" Kincade screamed.

"Oh, they did it alright. Then, Logan tried to make Whiskey Pete eat the meat. The boy said Whiskey Pete locked his mouth shut until his lips bled. The big fella—this Logan—put heavy leather gloves on and pulled a white hot stick from the campfire and waved it in front of Whiskey Pete, laughin' like some rabid wolf. Then he said, 'Time is over, Cookie, for you and for that friend 'a yours. I'll find Kincade. Roast him next. Good-bye, Cookie.' Then he jammed about a half-foot 'a that searing wood through Whiskey Pete's right eye. Went clear into his brain. That's exactly what happened. The boy swears it was just like that."

Kincade could stand no more. He bolted off the porch and leaped into the saddle without touching the stirrups. He pulled Gold Digger from the rail and sped like the wind down the street. Block after block of the town passed like leaves in a high wind. He bent low over the saddle horn and streaked across the country crazed, unable to slow down. As Gold Digger lathered, Kincade pulled himself up and came to a slow halt. With great effort he turned and headed back to Gypsy.

He found Boot Hill on the outskirts of town. He tied Digger to the picket fence and went through the open gate. There was only one new grave, still fresh with black earth. A simple marker stood at its head: "Whiskey Pete and Little Blue—a good man—a good dog."

Kincade fell to his knees, covered his face, and wailed. The lowest depths of purgatory could be no worse than this. "I swear on this grave, Logan, I'll never forget this, not till my dying day. I can look like a gunfighter, and sometimes I've been one. But I've always tried to avoid a showdown with you. No more. I'm coming for you, Logan. I'll blow your guts straight to hell. I'll never stop looking for you, not until vengeance is mine."

The confrontation of a lifetime was about to begin.

18

The saloon doors slammed open. Five men, looking like monstrous black bats straight out of hell, strode in. The snarl on their faces was somewhere between ferocious and jubilant. They looked dark. Not a hint of any color whatsoever. Simply dark . . . like shadows tucked into deep corners. Four of them headed for a small table near the back. The biggest and meanest-looking one went to the bar.

"Gimme two bottles, and they'd better be your best."

The shaking barkeep took two whiskey bottles from the shelf and put them on the bar. "That'll be . . . Never mind. Take whatever you want—on the house."

The leader tossed one bottle to a sidekick named Snake. "Pass it around." He kept the second for himself.

From the moment the five entered the saloon, those who had been gambling or drinking gradually slipped out the doors. "Well, well, look at that. We got the place all to ourselves. And here I was hoping to pick 'em off one by one like shootin' ducks in a pond." He pointed his finger like a gun at one table after another and then at the bar. "Bang! You're dead!" The bartender made a dash to the back room. This seemed very amusing to the four. They all cheered, and the one holding the bottle raised it in salute to Wil Logan.

Logan had organized his gang with himself at the top, of course. Below him were four handpicked *segundos*. He changed them from time to time, depending on their loyalty and ability to live. Occasionally more riders were recruited for bigger jobs. Logan confided in his "seconds" as little as possible. They were to follow his orders.

"So where is he, boss?" Snake asked. "Where's Kincade? Come on . . . let's find 'im and get on with this turkey shoot." The others snorted agreement.

There was quiet . . . what seemed an interminable quiet . . . as Logan looked at the four. "Don't have to find Kincade, Snake," said Logan finally.

"What?"

"I said we don't have to find him. He'll come to us. Which is a good thing, Snake. You couldn't even get hold of that damn cowdog before we roasted him, let alone handle somebody like Kincade. All we have to do is wait," snarled Logan.

"Here?" asked Snake.

"No."

"Where then?"

"We're gonna set a trap for him up Montana way." Spittle spewed down Logan's chin as he barked at Snake. "What I got planned in Montana is surefire. When we's done, Kincade'll be wolf bait, and we'll be rollin' in gold."

"How the hell is Kincade gonna know where we're waitin' for him in Montana?" Snake shot back.

"'Cause you're gonna tell him. After what we did in Benson and Gypsy, he's already trackin' me, you can be sure 'a that. All you gotta do is point him in the right direction. He'll drop into my trap like a plucked chicken in a pot."

Logan went to the bar and took five bottles of the good stuff from the stock in front of the mirror. "Drink up, boys. This is all workin' out better than I ever hoped."

"I don't think so, Logan." Snake slithered up from the table. The bandit next to him, a hard case named Buck Sloan, knew that in the next few seconds someone was going to have a window put in his skull.

"I'm more interested in Josephine than in this Kincade 'a yours. I couldn't care less about your boy. And I don't need you to introduce me to your Josie neither," hissed Snake, who drew his six-shooter and pointed it squarely at Logan's chest.

The volcanic fire deep within Logan's gut erupted. With a quick snap of his right hand, Logan withdrew the enormous Bowie knife from beneath his duster, and with a blurring motion threw it into the bone between Snake's eyes, burying the handle to the hilt. The outlaw's head opened like a floodgate, spewing brains and blood over the outlaws at his side. Snake's body shot over backward, landing with a thud on the barroom floor.

"Anybody else got any objections?" whispered Logan. Nobody moved. "Sloan, you'll be the one baitin' Kincade now. Snake's busy burnin' in hell."

19

Weeks passed as Kincade tracked Wil Logan, filled with the grief and guilt of Whiskey Pete's, Little Blue's, and Finley's deaths. He should have never left. With the Proud Cat incinerated, rumor was that Josephine was somewhere around Tombstone. Kincade was torn between his concern for Josephine's life and his hatred for Wil Logan. If Josie was in Tombstone, the marshal . . . Wyatt Earp . . . would see to her safety. Kincade would find Logan.

The old Indian had taught Kincade so well the gunfighter could follow a wood tick on solid rock. Logan's slime left a trail, and it led north toward Montana, covering hundreds of miles. Kincade's determination to find and kill Logan drove him forward. The time it would take was of little concern. This was a life quest for him.

His only respite was an occasional stop in a saloon to quickly rest and eat. Both were an elixir for the knot between his shoulder blades. Soft haze filling the room, the smell of tobacco, the give and take of men at the bar, the laughter of doves as their hands slowly caressed the necks of men bent over closely guarded fists full of playing cards. It all pulled him back from the abyss of losing his mind from his nearly uncontrollable anger. Kincade needed a good saloon, and he found one just after entering Montana.

Kincade took a table away from the doors, his back to the wall, and began the Wait. Looking toward the bar, Kincade nodded to himself ever so slightly. There was a large man seated with his wide back to Kincade. The big fellow's feet were as large as loading chutes, and his buckaroo boots were covered with dried cow manure. His spurs sported Mexican rowels as big as soup plates.

Kincade knew that this very large and very muscular fellow, seated on the fourth barstool from the right, had to be a working cowboy, big enough to stop a twenty-mule-team freight wagon.

The man hunkered down over a cold beer, with a pard at each side, left and right. The three probably had their barstools named after them, as comfortable and at home as they seemed.

Kincade continued the Wait, taking in table by table all those who filled the room. Halfway through his look-see, Kincade's eyes came to a dead stop. The knot between his shoulders retook its position quicker than the first rattler out of the box. There, not thirty feet away, staring at Kincade, was one of Logan's men. Kincade recognized him from the wanted posters: Buck Sloan.

Kincade's hands slowly left the tabletop, almost imperceptibly, landing on the grips of his pearl-handled Colts. His thumbs found the hammers.

Sloan picked up his glass, and took a pull, making absolutely sure that Kincade could see both his hands clearly. Pushing back his chair so slowly that it sent a scraping chill down the spines of those nearby, Buck Sloan stood, eyes never leaving Kincade, and began a measured walk straight toward the man Sloan knew was capable of killing him as dead as a can of corned beef.

"Take it easy, Kincade," Sloan said. "It wasn't me that set the fire in Benson."

Slowly, hands out front, easy to see, easy to judge, Buck Sloan continued to walk forward. Whether he was proud of it or not, Kincade knew what he had become: a gunfighter who could pull and fire twin smoke wagons with such lightning-fast accuracy and speed that any man who challenged him would be permanently driven into the ground like a stake. And that included Buck Sloan.

"And it wasn't me that planned the killin' of your pard at Gypsy neither," Sloan continued. "Just let me sit. I got somethin' you're gonna want to hear."

Kincade knew Sloan had snake blood in him and was tough enough to eat off the same plate as a diamondback rattler.

"Take it easy," Sloan said.

Sloan slowly pulled out the chair directly across the table from Kincade, knowing full well that the gunfighter's six-shooters were leveled at his gut. Lowering himself into the seat, Sloan kept both palms face down on the tabletop. He knew that if he so much as blinked wrong, Kincade would split his head like kindling.

"Word has it you been lookin' fer somebody we both know. You might be able to track a bear through running water," continued Sloan, "but I can save you a step or two."

Kincade was so focused on folding Sloan up like an empty purse that he was barely breathing.

"Full day's ride from here there's a mining town named Helena. Rough and tumble place." He wiped his cracked lips with the back of his hairy paw.

"There's a man waitin' fer you there, Kincade." Sloan moved his hands, palms up, as though about to give an offering, staring into Kincade's blue eyes. "That man is your Wil

Logan." And with that, a slight smile crept over Buck Sloan's ugly face, revealing a mouth full of crooked, chipped, and tobacco-stained teeth.

A thousand images flooded Kincade. Bile rose in his throat. His fists knotted around the pistol grips, his jaw clenched. For an instant he pictured the remains of the Proud Cat, imagined the screams from Finley as he was burned alive, and the agony Whiskey Pete felt seeing Little Blue skewered and broiled.

Kincade didn't return the smile. "Why are you telling me this? You're one of his men."

"*Wuz* one of 'em. Logan cheated me out of a payroll job. I've lit out on my own."

Slowly, deliberately, Kincade said, "You're a liar."

Sloan blinked. He knew that Kincade could sense treachery. Sloan's eyes were giving him away. Another slip like that and the bandit would be so full of lead he couldn't walk uphill. Sloan knew that Kincade wore his holsters tied down because when it came to business, the gunfighter didn't do much talking with his mouth.

"Take it easy . . ."

Kincade remained silent, watching Buck Sloan. The anger at that table completely stilled the room. Those in the saloon knew they were near enough to hell to smell smoke. One false move on the part of Buck Sloan, and Kincade would dig out his blue-lightning Colts and empty some cartridges.

Sloan spoke. "It wasn't me that tried to kill your Josephine."

That was the final straw.

Every man, every bar belle in the saloon froze. Every face looked at Kincade. At his eyes. The man was literally on fire. Kincade rose up to his full height, pushing the chair behind

him away with the tops of his boots. Then, with a sudden rise
of his right knee nearly to his chest, Kincade slingshot his
heel into the edge of the round table, sending it fifteen feet
across the room where it smashed into a wall, shattering into
pieces.

"Get up, you gutter trash." And Sloan did.

"You ever say her name again, I'll cut you in half."

Sloan didn't move.

"You're real close to dying, Sloan," Kincade whispered.
"You're standing at hell's gate." His eyes tore into Sloan, who
raised his arms out to each side, palms facing Kincade.

"Go on, you scum-sucking pig. Get yourself back to
Logan," said Kincade. "You tell him I'll see him . . . I'll see
him real soon."

Sloan backed up, slowly turned, and began to gradually
walk toward the saloon's front doors. Kincade drew his
hands away from the Colts, turning away from Sloan. And in
that split second, Logan's man withdrew a dagger from his
shirt, swirled toward Kincade, raising his arm to throw the
knife into Kincade's back.

At the same moment, the cowboy Kincade had been
watching leaped from his barstool and charged Sloan like
an enraged steer, crashing into Sloan, who plunged the
knife into the cowboy's beefy left shoulder. Kincade pivoted,
yanking his right six-shooter from its holster, bringing his
left palm down on the hammer while holding the trigger
down. In less than two seconds, Kincade fanned six slugs
into the skull of Buck Sloan, whose head exploded like a
melon.

He slowly returned the gun to its holster and walked over
to the cowboy, who was now kneeling on the floor. Kincade
removed the silk wildrag from his neck, placing it over the
knife wound. He helped the huge man to his feet.

"I owe you my life," Kincade said to the man.

"Aw . . . didn't seem fair, you gettin' it in the back," the cowboy smiled, placing his right hand over the kerchief to hold back the blood. "I've been speared a number of times by mean bulls when I wasn't lookin'."

The cowboy's simple comment allowed Kincade to breathe. The knot between his shoulders began to slowly loosen. "I'll bet," said Kincade. "But why is it that your enemies come with four legs and mine with two?" And Kincade smiled.

The two walked back to the bar. "Tequila, bartender. Beer alongside. And whatever my friend wants."

Helena, eh? Buck Sloan was a low-life, lying, sidewinder. But it might not hurt to head toward Helena.

20

Gold strikes turned the town of Helena, Montana, into a treasure trove. Smelters refined the ore into bars, and what wasn't processed there was packed into canvas bags spilling over with the glittering dust. These were loaded onto stagecoaches bound for the railheads at Corinne. Two burly shotgun riders rode atop each one of these stagecoaches, one seated next to the driver and the second astride the canvas sheet covering the luggage compartment. These were dangerous, highly trained guards, men who were hard as whetstones. They were paid well and expected to defend their cargoes without hesitation or fear.

Logan had watched the Wells Fargo stagecoaches come and go for weeks, learning their schedules, the loading process, and ways of each of the guards. He shadowed them as they traveled the road to Corinne, memorizing river crossings, the grades that slowed the horses to a crawl, the narrow sections, and way stations. He rode the valleys north and south, determining which offered the fastest escape to robbers.

Wil Logan was no ordinary bandit. Early in his youth, he had lost interest in looking for hogs to kick or store windows to break. The years had honed and refined his tastes for mayhem. Inflicting pain on others fueled him, and doing it had become as easy as licking butter off a knife. It wasn't just the money, though Logan had stolen and squandered enormous amounts of it over the years. It was the thrill of terrorizing the souls of others that gave Logan a reason for living. The man had become utterly depraved and fearless of death. He had been its instrument for years.

Logan's years of lawlessness had also made him cunning. He had no intention of rotting in some jail like other bandits he had crossed paths with who pretended to know what they were doing but in reality were so dumb they couldn't hit a bull in the butt with a bass fiddle. No, Wil Logan was weasel smart. He took his time trolling the back alleys of Helena, finding exactly the right gunmen to replace Snake and Buck Sloan.

When Logan first hatched his plan, it was only to rob a stagecoach. But since Josephine's escape in Benson, and Whiskey Pete's refusal to give up Kincade, he had come up with a scheme that boiled with malevolent pleasure. His robbery of the Wells Fargo stage to Corinne would get Kincade killed, either by Logan or by a shotgun rider.

Kincade had always wanted to do the right thing—a fatal weakness in Logan's estimation. That weakness would assure Logan's own clean getaway after robbing the stage to Corinne. Wil Logan was ready to make his move on the morning of July the eighth.

Logan knew that when Kincade first entered Helena, he would hit the best saloon. Not only because such places boiled with information, but because saloons were Kincade's weakness. Logan told a couple of booze-blinded saddle tramps that drinks would be on him and to tell any tall, two-gun stranger there was a rumor that Logan and his gang were laying in ambush for the stage. Word was the robbery would take place around noon as the stage neared Corinne that very same day. It was as easy as handing Kincade an engraved invitation to a barn dance. He would take the bait surefire.

The trick was for Logan and his men to pick off the two guards while they were sitting on their gun hands and get the stage stopped. Two of the segundos would take care of the driver and passengers while the other two loaded the gold into saddlebags. They all would make sure that the travelers overheard them giving full credit for the holdup to their boss, a gunfighter named Kincade, who was certain to be riding up at any moment.

And once he did show up, Logan himself would put a bullet into Kincade, claiming the money for himself and the rest of the gang.

But from where the passengers sat and from the chatter they had overheard, it would be their leader, Kincade, who had masterminded the robbery from the start. It would be too bad that the rest of the scum had gotten away, but with Kincade dead in the dirt, at least the Wells Fargo Stage Company could have some satisfaction in the death of their leader.

It all would have worked, just as Logan had planned, had the one lady passenger not gotten all high and mighty, telling the robbers they were sure to burn in hell for what they were doing. Listening to psalms and exhortations on sin wasn't Wil Logan's bowl of soup.

Which is why Logan had that very same lady yanked back by the neck with his right hand, tearing her blouse away with his left as he sadistically howled with pleasure, just as Kincade rode over the rise near Corinne at a full gallop.

Gold Digger could run like the wind. That speed nearly

caused Kincade to trample the body of a large man sprawled in the road, whose right chest was completely missing from an enormous gunshot wound, probably from a twelve-gauge scattergun.

Ahead, Kincade could see the Wells Fargo coach, the driver's hands held high. Another man was hanging backward off the rear of the coach, his feet tangled in the canvas, half of his head blown off. At the side of the road, two rather well-dressed men with their hands above their heads followed the orders of two masked bandits. Two others of the gang were heaving the gold shipment from the stage. A fifth outlaw stood behind a woman, obviously a passenger, who desperately struggled against the huge arm of the man choking the life from her.

Kincade took it all in within two seconds as Gold Digger charged forward. But something didn't make sense.

Why weren't they shooting at him? The lot of them should be scattering like roaches. But no, it was almost as though they were waiting for Kincade to join them in completing the stickup. He released both hammer tie-downs in order to jerk both pistols the moment Gold Digger pulled up short.

Amazingly, three of the bandits turned to him, waving their hands as though all of them were good friends. "Kincade, what took you so long?" said one. "You got here just in time," said a second. "Boss, you planned this one perfect," said a third.

As Kincade approached, the passengers and driver looked at him with eyes filled with fear, not of the robbery they were smack in the midst of, but of Kincade himself. It was as if each of them believed they were seconds away from Kincade skinning their flesh.

The fifth outlaw spun the female passenger in order to bring her body between Kincade's and his own, leveling his own six-shooter up and under the jaw of the woman. "Change of plans, Kincade. This may have been your robbery, but we're taking the money for ourselves."

"Logan!" Kincade pulled his left six-gun, pointing it straight at the man. "Let her go!"

Logan yanked her head back, and the scum discharged his pistol into the woman's throat. The shock of seeing her brutal murder stopped Kincade, and in those two missing seconds, Logan recocked his pistol and put his next bullet squarely into Kincade's left shoulder. The tremendous impact twisted Kincade backward, the lead hotter than the hubs of hell. Gold Digger reared up, hooves flailing at the air.

Logan dropped the woman, foam now spewing from her missing jaw, leaped to his horse, and spurred, the rest of his gang hot on his heels.

"You!" yelled the stage driver. "You'll get yours, Kincade!" He yanked a rifle from beneath the coach seat, and fanned the lever in an attempt to rack and fire.

"No! I wasn't . . ." Kincade regained control of Gold Digger just as the driver let a round fly past Kincade's head. A quick snap of his wrist, and the Wells Fargo man prepared to fire a second round. Spinning Digger, Kincade jammed his spurs deep into the stallion's sides, and the horse charged after Logan and his men. Three more rifle shots whined past Kincade's head. A fourth slammed into a tree, shattering a limb into pieces as Gold Digger galloped beneath.

The wound in Kincade's shoulder felt like a white-hot branding iron had been pressed into the bone. He bent low over the saddle horn, letting his palomino run like the wind.

But Logan and his men were gone. No chance to catch and bring them back. Now it was Kincade who would be accused of masterminding the Wells Fargo stagecoach robbery east of Helena near a little town called Corinne, Montana.

Logan's planned double-cross had worked. Kincade was alive, but running for his life.

The white-hot sun scorched the rimrock one last time before making its retreat below the western horizon. Off to the east a dust devil swirled up, whipping the mesquite, suddenly choking off the diminishing rays of the setting sun and filtering its remains into smoky shafts of light.

Something green and loathsome crawled onto a nearby boulder, its forked tongue smelling the air.

Kincade's eyes snapped open. Had he fallen asleep from exhaustion or passed out from pain? Either way, he must guard against it happening again.

He raised himself on one elbow. God, how that hurt! His deep blue eyes slowly scanned the horizon. No sign of riders. The sheriff's posse tracking him must have been fooled when he crossed the slick rock and doubled back into the arroyo. He collapsed back onto the sand and slowly closed his eyes again. He couldn't have been out long, for the coals of the campfire he had struggled to build had just reached the temperature for the job that had to be done.

The searing pain in his left shoulder triggered an involuntary grinding of teeth and clenching of fists. How bad was it? He tore open his bloodied shirt, which was caked with red soil, and stared at the wound. He had seen bullet holes that were smaller and bigger but none that appeared more fatal. Blood oozed from the torn flesh. Kincade knew if he didn't get that bullet out he would die.

What's it gonna be, Kincade? he thought to himself. You can't get Logan if your bones are bleaching in this desert. Get on with it.

Kincade whistled to his palomino, Gold Digger, who obediently trotted to his side. He grimaced as he pulled down the worn saddlebags and rummaged inside for the surgeon's tool. The instrument, once shiny but now blackened with use, measured a foot long. One end held two steel ovals, the first for a thumb, and the second for an index finger—much like a pair of seamstress scissors. At the other end of the shaft, two tiny claws faced each other, each half the size of one of the buttons on Kincade's shirt. The surgeon's tool was meant to probe, to root around, and to grab hold. He had used it on others, but this would be the first time he had tried it on himself.

Kincade jammed the device into the red-hot coals of the campfire. Whatever microscopic bugs made their home on that steel were now in the process of meeting their maker. As the coals crackled, the green reptile scurried across the boulder, disappearing into a deep crack. Within minutes, the steel glowed with the same heat and intensity as the fire itself.

Reaching out with his right hand, Kincade slowly withdrew the tool from the glowing embers, throwing a small shower of sparks. He opened the claws to the width of a .45-caliber Colt slug. With his left hand, Kincade jammed the rein of Gold Digger's bridle between his jaws, and bit down hard.

Damn Logan, thought Kincade. Damn him to hell. His hatred of his mortal enemy was now deeper, uglier, more vicious than the bullet that hid three inches beneath his skin where it had slammed into the bone. But this was not the time for revenge. It would come; Kincade promised himself . . . it would come.

Seconds after the twin claws disappeared into the jagged wound, moments after Kincade's teeth bit deep into the latigo, Gold Digger's nostrils flared wide at the smell of burning flesh. The palomino's head instinctively jerked back. But not a sound came from Kincade as the probe went deeper, seeking Logan's bullet, its lead head now flared from target impact.

The claw hands bumped into the spent bullet, nudging it deeper into the wound by a fraction of an inch, just enough to send any man into convulsions. But not Kincade. The hate-filled fire in his gut for what Wil Logan had done to him far outstripped the unimaginable pain now coursing through his left shoulder.

His fingers parted, the claws parted, the fingers closed, the claws closed, and the disfigured bullet began to be drawn out of the torn muscle. The palomino jerked again as the smell became even stronger.

And then it was out.

Kincade spat the rein from his mouth, dropped the tool, and with his right hand reached for and cracked open the container of spoiled meat that had been in his saddlebags one week too long. He jammed his fingers into a squirming knot of freshly hatched white maggots, retrieving a palm-sized colony, brought the nest across his chest, and spilled the wriggling mass of larvae into the open bullet wound. The grubs would clean the gash, just as the old Indian had taught him so long ago.

The sun disappeared. The light shafts vaporized. The air went still.

"You've slowed me, but you haven't stopped me. I'll get you, Logan. If it's the last thing I do, I'll get you."

Kincade blacked out . . .

21

Logan and his segundos were in high spirits as they rode away from Corinne. They didn't stop until a secluded grove of trees afforded them protection to divide the loot they had stowed away in their saddlebags.

"Here's your share," said Logan. "I'm keepin' half 'cause it was my idea. But there's plenty left over for you boys to split."

Under their breath the four grumbled, but letting Logan know would be like signing their own death warrants. Only Chico Fernandez, who had been with Logan the longest, dared a criticism.

"Thought you was gonna kill Kincade."

"Leavin' him in the dirt to take all the blame is even better, you dummy. Now he's wanted dead or alive. I'm only sorry I won't be there to see him hang."

"Right," Chico agreed nervously. "You're always right, Wil."

As was his habit, Logan put his finger alongside his right nostril, inhaled deeply, and blew a glob of snot onto the ground. "Mount up. We've wasted enough time here. Let's toss around some of that Montana gold we're packin'. Another two hours of ridin', and we'll all be gamblin' and drinkin' and whorin'."

The four cheered, and they all swung into their saddles eager to let the Corinne affair be forgotten.

Silver Spike was a town that had appeared out of nowhere because those who built the railroad had to have a place to spend their wages. In time it changed from a hell-on-wheels working-class camp to a respectable community of business and trades people and one that welcomed settlers and travelers.

The Logan gang sized up the town as they rode in. Folks had put up wood houses, some with curtains in the parlor windows and flowers planted in the yards. The stores had glass fronts for looking inside. Three restaurants sported large sandwich boards by their doors to ballyhoo their specialties. There were two churches, both with steeples.

All in all, Silver Spike was not the kind of town that catered to the likes of Logan and his cohorts. The gang felt edgy to find a saloon and get on with the celebrating.

As they rode farther they came upon a red schoolhouse. Younger boys and girls were in recess while older students labored inside. The children were laughing and playing simple games. There was a teeter-totter and a tipped-over molasses barrel for hide and seek. A willow tree stood out front. A frayed rope tied to a high and sturdy limb held a wooden swing the size of a dinner plate on its opposite end.

As Logan approached, he felt the anger and jealousy of his own childhood boil up. Drawing his pistol, he fired at the swing, shattering the wooden seat into pieces.

The children screamed and began running back to the schoolhouse.

"Let's round 'em up, boys!" Logan shouted, and he cut his horse back and forth to chase the frightened youngsters. His gang followed in pursuit, laughing and shouting, viciously reining their mounts, which snorted and whinnied and tore up the dirt.

The schoolmarm and older students rushed to the window and, seeing the mayhem, the teacher dashed out the door. Like a mother hen gathering her chicks under her wings, she rushed hither and thither, arms flailing, trying to protect and direct the youngest ones.

"Inside, darlings! Hurry! Hurry!" This only made the five rogues laugh and ride harder.

When all the children were finally safe in the schoolhouse, she stood at the door and shook her fist at Logan's men. "You beasts!" she shouted. "Leave—you hear me? Leave before I call the sheriff!"

Logan pulled to a stop right in front of her and reared his horse on its hind legs, the front hooves pawing the air. "Just how you think you're gonna call the sheriff when we got you surrounded?" he bellowed. Then he winked. "Give me a kiss, Teacher, and we'll be on our way."

The schoolmarm looked horrified. She turned, slamming and bolting the door behind her.

Logan swung off his horse and mounted the steps. With one big kick he smashed open the door. He grabbed the terrified lady. "I said give me a kiss!"

He threw her back and planted his fat, wet lips tight on hers, his greasy mustache stuffed up her nose. She fainted. He dropped her to the floor and stormed out as the frightened children ran to her side.

"Come on, boys. I got what I was after. I'm hungry. Let's get some grub." They galloped down the street with the sounds of loud weeping coming from the schoolhouse.

"That was fun," the four were saying, but Logan was grim as he looked for the nearest saloon that served food.

"God, I hate kids," he said as he slumped into a chair at a big round table. "Snot-nose show-offs. Think they're smarter'n me just 'cause they can read and write and do figurin'. If I had my way they'd all be lined up and turned into a shootin' gallery." He pointed his finger like a gun. "Bang! Bang! Bang! Runts are good for nothin' but target practice."

"Place your order, gents," a man behind the bar said.

Logan looked questioningly at the four who shrugged. "Steak, eggs, 'taters, pie. And five beers while we're waitin." The mugs were brought to the table, and Logan took a long swig, wiping his mouth with the back of his hand. He sighed and grinned.

"You know, I went to school once—one day that is." They laughed and saluted their mugs to him. "Teacher told me never to come back again just 'cause I stole a kid's lunch pail and beat him up when he tried to get it back."

Logan picked up his mug, twisting it in his hands. "Kincade can read, you know. That same teacher gave him lessons after school in her own house." He downed the last of the brew and slammed the mug hard enough to break it

"Bring me another! And hurry up with that grub!" he shouted toward the bar.

Chico Fernandez gulped his beer and gave a silly laugh. "Then Kincade won't have no trouble readin' those wanted posters with his name in big letters: KINCADE DEAD OR ALIVE."

Logan guffawed and slapped him on the back. "You got that right, pard."

Chico gave a silent sigh of relief. The crisis was past. "Where we gonna go now, Wil?"

"Well, I been thinkin' Colorado. Ain't been there for awhile so it's ripe for our pickin'. Okay with you boys?" He looked at the four, and they all nodded. "I thought so. You idiots never had a plan of your own in your whole lives."

The food was placed on the table. "That'll be twenty dollars."

Logan tossed the barkeep a gold piece. "Where do we find the cheapest whores in town?" Then, a sick smile crossed his face. "Hey, where's that schoolteacher live?"

22

Kincade slowly made his way back to the Sabin ranch. The owner welcomed him like a son. Of course he could stay there while his wound healed.

"There are a lot of chores I can still do, Mr. Sabin, and I'm eager to get back the full use of my arm."

"I'll keep you busy. Get your gear into the bunkhouse, and welcome home."

The old nightmare of young Wil Logan slashing Kincade's throat was joined by two others that haunted him nearly every night. In one Whiskey Pete was being roasted on a spit over a huge fire, and Logan was trying to make Little Blue eat the flesh. In the other Logan lashed Josephine to the front of the Proud Cat, setting her on fire, howling from the street as she writhed in agony.

The first time Kincade had one of these nightmares in the bunkhouse he woke up screaming. The other hands knew that Kincade was recovering from a bullet wound, and that his nightmares had to be part of it. But Kincade knew he would have to sleep somewhere by himself. He moved his bedroll into the stable and slept by Gold Digger. His only recourse after a nightmare was to swing onto his horse bareback, lean over the warmth of Digger's neck, and hang onto the silky mane. They would walk quietly around the yard until Kincade calmed down and could return to the stable. It was pure hell—over and over again.

One of Kincade's jobs was to go to the post office in the nearest town to send and pick up mail for the ranch. He would pull his hat low over his brow and keep to himself, never mentioning his own name to others. Wanted posters lined the walls of the front entry, and Kincade knew that his own face would soon join the gallery of rogues. One wall held the worst of the lot, the killers wanted dead or alive. An entire row was filled with grainy photos of Wil Logan, and grisly accounts of the horrific crimes he had committed. One poster told the story of a desperate father looking for his kidnapped daughter. "Five-hundred-dollar reward for the return of six-year-old Melissa Wilcox, believed to have been abducted by Wil Logan outside of Julesburg, Colorado, this July." Kincade shook his head in disgust. That would have meant that Logan had taken the little girl after the Montana stage robbery where Kincade had been shot. Would the man's thirst for blood never end?

By late August, Kincade's shoulder was almost like new. His ability to pull both six-shooters with blazing accuracy and speed not only returned, but were even better than before he had taken Logan's bullet. Sabin approached him toward the end of the month. "You goin' on the fall drive with us, Kincade? We're headin' for Benson, and that was a favorite stomping ground of yours."

"Not any more, Mr. Sabin. What I liked best there is gone. But I'll go as far southwest as you're headed, if that's all right."

"I need you on drag."

"What other spot is there?"

So Kincade and Gold Digger once again entered the world of choking dust and bawling cattle. On the trail he became lost in memories, consuming him with anger. He would ride for miles thinking about the devastation at Benson, the atrocity at Gypsy, the deadly robbery and double-cross outside of Corinne.

Sometimes at the end of a day he had no idea where he was or how he had gotten there. He wondered if he had herded cattle at all that day, or was he just riding on Digger in search of Logan. But no one reprimanded him for his work so he must have done what was necessary without thinking. The herd moved too slowly for him. The days passed in torment. He was eager to start his search for Logan once again.

When Mr. Sabin paid Kincade his final wages, he held out his hand. "I know what you're gonna do now, and I don't blame you. Good luck finding this Logan."

"I appreciate what you've done for me."

"Well, if you ever want to come back, the job's open."

Kincade smiled at Sabin, appreciating the offer. "Probably not. When I get this thing with Logan settled, I might go into the saloon business in Tombstone. There's a partnership waiting, and she's a lot prettier than you."

Sabin laughed. "S'long, Kincade." They rode off in opposite directions.

Logan's trail was laid out by the wanted posters showing up in more and more post offices across the West. The gang had ridden south from Montana and into Colorado, where the Wilcox girl had been kidnapped. From there, another stage holdup and rape in Fort Garland; wanted for murder in Santa Fe; wanted for pillage and burning in Silver City; wanted for bank robbery in Cochise. Logan and his badmen were heading southwest to Arizona Territory. But even without the posters, Kincade knew that Wil Logan was bound for Tombstone. If the scum had Josephine, he had Kincade.

Kincade never saw a wanted flyer for himself, but he knew they were beginning to appear. As he rode southwest following Logan's path of destruction, he would hear his name in saloons. "Oh yeah, Kincade," he would hear. "He's the fella that shot Buck Sloan" or "He's the man that robbed the Wells Fargo outside 'a Corinne where that lady got killed . . . rode away with his gang afterwards." Since he always wore his two-gun rig, men would eye Kincade carefully and keep their distance.

But at a saloon on the border of the Arizona Territory an encounter took place that would change Kincade's life.

23

It happened in Chiricahua.

That day Kincade had ridden fourteen hours. After seeing to Gold Digger, he headed for the town saloon. He stepped up to the bar and leaned onto the weathered top. "Two fingers of that mescal you have there behind you. 'N a beer."

Kincade watched the golden liquid fill his glass, anticipating the warmth in his veins. Looking into the mirrored glass of the back bar, Kincade began the Wait, letting his eyes come to rest on each patron one by one, learning, sizing up, and watching. It was as though Kincade was drinking in people so he could get a read on staying, or leaving. More than once, Kincade had discovered cruelty and deception in people's hearts. The Wait always revealed them. That was the biggest reason Kincade would never stop his search for Wil Logan. He reeked of both.

Kincade slowly raised the shot glass, letting the tequila barely touch his lips, looking over the rim and into the mirror's reflection, searching for signs of Logan or any of his gang. Across the room, two men sat playing cards.

"Hey, mister, you in or out?" the one dealing asked. It had been a heated game ever since this gunman had come in an hour earlier. The man's eyes bored into the dealer's skull, reading the dealer's intentions as clearly as through he was looking directly at his cards. Then the gunman looked over the dealer's shoulder to the bar. The hair went up on the back of his neck. If the shot glass in his right hand were any less stout, he would have smashed the thing without even knowing it.

"I don't believe it. It's Kincade, in the flesh!" the man said to himself. Without thinking, he fingered his six-shooters like they were his second skin.

"Hey, you in or out?" asked the one with the deck, as his armpits filled with the sweaty anticipation of losing his shirt.

Even though the length of the two players' relationship had been limited to just over sixty minutes, the dealer's question was tempered with a great deal of restraint. He had already surmised that no sane person would ever treat this man with anything but respect. Not unless that person wanted to be plowed six feet under in less than three seconds.

Kincade, so you've found your way here, thought the gunman. I wonder how your bullet wound healed, after what happened to you up in Montana. He slowly spun the shot glass in his right hand. "I'll sit out a hand," he told the dealer. He shoved his chair back a foot or two, and leaned back to watch Kincade who was talking to a cowboy who had just come in from the street. "I wonder if that fella knows who he's mixing up with." The man smiled to himself.

The saloon's card dealer felt the intense stare of the man across from him, now directed toward Kincade. The gunman stood up from the table, keeping his eyes fixed on Kincade. The dealer had seen eyes like that before. They were reserved for those who had evolved into skilled predators. But he hushed his mouth, frightened to say, or even think, anything further.

Fear began to extend beyond their table. As intoxicated as many of the saloon's customers were, they too began to watch this young shooter, festooned in a bullet-filled gunbelt that held a blued six-shooter jammed behind it. He just stood there, staring at Kincade from across the room. All could see that the man's body was rigid, almost frozen, engrossed in Kincade's every move.

Like a small break in an earthen dam, discomfort began to flow through the crowd as more and more of them became aware of the gunman's fascination with Kincade, wondering what the intentions of the young cowboy were. They were about to find out.

Kincade placed both his hands flat on the bar and continued to stare straight ahead, beyond the rows of bottles and into the mirror behind. Crossing to Kincade's left, the stranger approached the bar. Man by man, he moved closer to Kincade. Some of the customers made a hurried exit out the saloon's front door. Others who were seated quietly placed their pistols in their laps, figuring if lead was going to fly between the two of them, they had best be ready.

The young gunman moved closer still, until he was side by side, no more than a whisper away from Kincade. A floorboard creaked, ever so slightly, at his feet.

"Jess . . ." said Kincade, his eyes still fixed on the back bar's mirror, "one of these days, I'm going to have to send you to charm school. Walking lightly was never your forte."

Jesse Keller smiled and shook his head, realizing that once again, Kincade had him cold. "Hello, Kincade. It's been too long."

"Never too long for blood brothers." And the two men embraced in an alliance that had lasted since childhood.

"Jess, have you looked around this room?" asked Kincade

quietly. "There are more shooters ready to split you up the backside then there are spines on prickly pear cactus."

"And here I'm such a nice guy," said Jesse.

"Well then, you owe these nervous folks an apology."

"You're right. I may be upsetting some stomachs as we speak."

Kincade reached for the bottle of mescal, pouring himself another finger or two. "Go ahead, Jess," Kincade said, taking another sip. "I'm interested to see how you tell all these folks in here that you're such a nice guy. Let's see how you go about it."

Jesse shook his head. "I . . . uh . . . may need some help. Remember, I ain't gone to no charm school."

Kincade laughed. "Oh hell, do I have to get you outta every mess you get yourself into?" Kincade raised his right eyebrow, winked at Jesse, and turned to also face the room. "Please excuse my young friend here. He doesn't get to town much, notably cities as cultured at Chiricahua. I assure you that he's a good boy, and here solely to lose what money he has to the tables and the drink of your fine community."

Kincade turned and whispered to Jesse. "Smile and tip your hat to 'em."

Jesse smiled and tipped his hat.

"That's better," said Kincade, slapping Jesse on the back.

While Kincade knew that Jesse would like to wrestle him to the ground for saying such things, Jess kept his eyes forward, offering a pearly white smile to all in the room, rolling his shoulders up in kind of an "aw shucks" manner. Within moments, the room relaxed, the piano started up, and the chatter recommenced as though nothing had happened. Two dozen pistols returned to their holsters.

"You said I was a good boy?" Jesse poked his nose into Kincade's face.

"You're right," said Kincade. "I probably was too nice."

Jesse shook his head, realizing that Kincade was having tremendous fun at his expense. "How'd you know it was me?"

"'Cause you're so little and skinny. How'd you know it was me?"

"'Cause you're so big and ugly." They both laughed. "Kincade, I can't believe I'm lucky enough to see your miserable face again. Buy me a drink, will ya?" said Jesse, snatching the tequila bottle from the bar.

"Use a glass, will ya?" laughed Kincade. "You're in a town of culture."

"You bet, real classy." And Jesse slapped Kincade on the back, hard enough to knock the wind out of him. "And you know what, Kincade? I've always thought you're a classy fella too." They both returned to face the bar, lowering their voices.

"Jess," said Kincade, "somethin' happened up in Montana, on the road between Helena and Corinne. I'll never be able to make it right. But I will make the scum responsible pay."

"I know about Logan, Kincade. I heard about that robbery and have a hunch as to what really happened," said Jesse. "I even seen your face on a wanted for armed robbery poster in the last town I rode through."

Jesse could see Kincade visibly tense as though he had struck a raw nerve. It was a mistake to mention the wanted poster. Jesse quickly did what he could to heal the now open wound. "I don't know where they got that picture of you, Kincade. But when we're done with Wil, we'd best bump off that photographer next." Kincade's smile returned. "You have enough trouble attracting the ladies as it is." The tension eased.

Kincade spoke again. "Jess, Logan has rounded up the dregs of the Southwest for that gang 'a his."

"Was Sloan one of 'em?"

"I met him once. The others are worse. Much worse," said Kincade. "Killing is not only their business, it's their pleasure. They thrill to the pain of others. Logan's gang is not fit to breathe."

"Then we'll just have to take the breath outta them," said Jesse.

Kincade looked deeply into his friend's eyes. He paused, and then said, "Logan is my fight."

"Our fight, Kincade," Jesse quickly followed. "Our fight."

It was immediately apparent to Kincade that Jesse wasn't about to budge on the matter. For better or worse, they would ride together.

Better for Kincade. Worse . . . much worse . . . for Logan.

24

The next morning, before checking out of the Chiricahua Hotel, Kincade got a bath and a shave and ate a breakfast of T-bone steak, six eggs, and what the cook called Indian bread but which bore no resemblance to Whiskey Pete's. He downed a bucket of black coffee.

"Mornin', Mr. Kincade," beamed the young desk clerk, accepting Kincade's room key.

"Mornin'," replied Kincade, "I'd like to settle up."

"Yes sir, Mr. Kincade!" the clerk beamed. "Did you sleep well?"

Kincade waited silently for his bill.

"I myself feel wonderful today!" offered the clerk. "Slept like a baby last night . . . like a newborn baby!"

"I can see that," said Kincade, getting a little impatient. Then he thought how gracious Josephine always was to everyone, so he added, "Perky, I would call it."

"Wonderfully perky!" echoed the clerk.

Somebody tapped Kincade from behind on the left shoulder. Kincade jerked. "Dang it, Jess. Cough or somethin' before you sneak up on me like that."

Jesse coughed.

"Before you get up behind me, not after."

"Oh," smiled Jesse.

After settling the hotel bill, the two men walked into the street, turned left and down to the livery where Gold Digger had been stabled. "Mister," said the boy mucking out stalls, "that's one mean horse you got there."

"Keep your voice down, son," Kincade said. "Gold Digger hear you say that, it might make him cranky." And Kincade walked into the barn to get the palomino from his stall as the boy's eyes grew wide.

Jesse, who had already retrieved and saddled his appaloosa, stood in the street, reins in hand, twirling the ends so they would smack into his left glove with a gentle but distinct pop. Kincade emerged from the barn and mounted up, his gear lashed to the saddle. His Winchester 73 faced forward in the scabbard, the butt easily within reach in front of the right knee, encircled by Kincade's riata.

Jesse stood in the dirt, paused, and then looked up at Kincade. "Want me to cough again?"

"Funny, Jess."

Jesse thought so too. He swung up and onto his saddle, completely bypassing the stirrup. "This here's Left Hand Man—a good horse."

"Mornin', Lefty."

"Where we headed? I been lookin' for you, not Logan."

"I figure he's headed for Tombstone. There's a lady has a saloon there. He tried to destroy her twice before. He'll try it again just to get at me. Except this time, I'll be there."

"Well, you know, Kincade. I myself kinda feel like headin' south. Tombstone maybe. That sit alright with you?"

Kincade shook his head to himself as Jesse's eyes twinkled. "Let's go . . ."

For the first two hours of the ride, Kincade kept his

thoughts to himself, knowing what undoubtedly lay ahead in Tombstone. Logan and his gang not only outnumbered them, but their skills at killing far exceeded Kincade's and Jesse's. He finally broke the silence. "You sure you want to stick with me, Jess? This could be our last ride, together or alone."

"You my blood brother or not?"

"Yeah, I know—forever and ever. But when you're lying in some back alley in Tombstone with your guts spillin' out all over the ground, don't say I never gave you a chance to back out."

"You're makin' me look forward to Tombstone more and more, pard. Got any other pictures you'd like to paint of my future?"

"Yeah. You're gonna be the loser when I beat you racin' to the top of that next rise. Hyahh, Digger!" And Kincade took off like a shot, followed closely by Left Hand Man. They raced with the wind and finished in a tie at the top of the hill.

"Damn, Kincade. I thought Left Hand was the best."

"Second best. But we'll try again when they cool down."

The days that followed were filled with friendly competition. "I bet Lefty can barrel through those bushes faster than Digger."

"On that plow horse you haven't got a chance."

Another day they sat on their mounts as they let them drink from a fast-flowing stream. Jesse said, "I'll be in the water 'fore you are." He slid from his horse as Kincade cleared the saddle.

"I'll swim to the other side 'fore you're out of your drawers."

Both men splashed and floundered in the swift current, laughing out loud, and remembering much simpler times.

"So you won on this side, but I'll beat you goin' back."
They both jumped in together, laughing twice as hard.

The warm sun felt good as they lay exhausted on their
bedrolls. Kincade looked at Jesse's arm. "Still got that 'K'
scar, I see."

"Still got that Indian bag around your neck, I see."

"Some things never change."

"Not the things that really matter."

They were only a day's ride out of Tombstone. They had
finished the last of the baked beans, and Jesse was juggling
the empty can back and forth in his hands. "Bet my draw is
faster than yours," he said.

"I'll call you on that. You don't know who you're dealin'
with, kid."

Taking turns, they tossed the can, shooting at it from the
hip. First they tossed it straight up. Then to one side and the
other, and even behind so they would have to turn as they
fired. The can spun and flipped as each bullet hit. If a bullet
ricocheted off the can, making it start to fall, the other shooter would hit it dead center. Neither of them ever missed.

"Damn, you're good, Jess. Who taught you to shoot? It
wasn't me."

Jesse picked up the battered can and heaved it as far as he
could. "I was gonna wait for a good time to tell you. I guess
this is as good as any."

"Tell me what?"

"I'm gonna tell you something you might not like."

"If it's coming from you, I'll not take it unkindly."

"Just remember that." Jesse squatted down on his haunch-
es, and Kincade joined him. "I really missed you after you
left for the ranches. Young buck that I was, I was so lonely.
But then Wil Logan started bein' real nice to me."

Kincade's jaw tightened.

"I think maybe he was hopin' I'd tell him where you went. But I didn't know and wouldn't have told him if I had known."

Kincade fell quiet, wondering what was coming next.

"Wil taught me to shoot a gun. And when he started formin' his gang, he asked me to go with him."

Kincade's head recoiled. "Pretty rough company." Kincade's voice had an edge to it.

"That's exactly what Miz Agnes Johnson said. You remember the widow woman I was livin' with?" Kincade nodded. "Well, she carried on somethin' awful when I told her what I was gonna do. She cried and twisted her apron and had to sit down. She told me some awful things about Wil—things he'd done that I didn't know about. She called him the son of Satan. There was even somethin' so unbelievable that I thought she was making it up, but she swore it was true."

"Why didn't you pay attention to her?"

"Oh hell, Kincade, she'd never paid me no mind before. How come all of a sudden she feels responsible for me? I was just a kid, and Wil's gang seemed more like an adventure than anything dangerous or ugly. I found out she was right before long."

"You went along with what Logan was doing?"

"I've done some things that I'm ashamed of, but I never got brutal. I decided to quit the gang when Logan started going completely loco about gettin' you. I told him I wanted no part of anything that would hurt you. He got so angry it was like he was comin' apart. Told me I was a traitor, that he'd taught me everything I knew, and that you'd just run off and left me.

"I told him I'd had enough. Told him he was crazy." Jesse paused. "He tried to shoot me! I ran out to Lefty and high-tailed it. He was yellin' he'd kill me dead fer sure if he ever caught me ridin' with you."

Kincade looked hard into Jesse's eyes. "Were you part of the burning of the Proud Cat and the killing of my pard, Whiskey Pete?"

"No."

"Did you have anything to do with the stage robbery at Corinne?"

"Hell no, Kincade. That was planned after I left. But I know all about it from two of his gang that got drunk in a saloon I was in. They was braggin' about it." Jesse slowly twirled a twig between his two fingers, looking at Kincade without blinking.

Kincade sat silently, thinking about what Jesse had revealed. Finally, he picked up a stone and threw it in the river. "How come you didn't tell me this before now, Jess?"

"Maybe I was testin' our friendship to see if it was strong enough for somethin' like this. It's been a long time since we was together. I thought maybe you'd changed—maybe I'd changed too much. There's got to be a right time to tell somethin'—especially if it's important. Right now seemed like the right time." Jesse broke the twig in half. "You sore at me?"

Silence.

"You still my blood brother, Kincade?" There was something almost wistful in Jesse's voice. Kincade could see that his friend felt cut to the core for what he had done.

Kincade paused, then said, "I know what it feels like to be lonely, Jess. I understand why you did what you did. Forget it."

He walked over to his friend, putting his hand on Jesse's shoulder. "Thanks for tellin' me."

Come nightfall, after seeing to their horses, Jesse gathered wood for a fire while Kincade placed their gear close to a ring of rocks he had arranged to hold back the hot coals. Now, with an even deeper feeling of brotherhood, Jesse told

Kincade that his picture was showing up on Wells Fargo posters across the Southwest. But he wasn't wanted just for robbery. He was accused of being the leader of a gang of killers. He was wanted dead or alive.

Kincade thought of the Corinne stage robbery, and Logan's hideous laugh after the murder of the woman passenger. Because of Logan's trick, Kincade might be running for the rest of his life, or what was left of it after the bounty hunters started up. Some of them were such skilled trackers they could hunt a whisper in a big wind. And if he wasn't killed outright, he could end up spending thirty years behind bars, rotting in some prison hellhole.

Kincade knotted his hands and looked at Jesse who sat watching Kincade near the firelight.

"For the life of me," said Kincade, "I can't understand why you'd want part of this mess. You may be forty-eight hours away from a firefight unlike anything even you have fought your way into or out of."

Jesse looked at Kincade without speaking.

"Our fight you say," Kincade continued, his voice rising. "You always were blind loyal, Jess. You owe it to yourself to get out of here, and if you got a lick of sense, you'll do it here and now."

Jesse flipped a twig into the fire, sending a small shower of sparks into the dark sky.

"Give me one good reason why you think you're gonna get out of a ride into damnation, Jess."

Jesse stared at his lifelong friend for nearly a minute without speaking, their eyes locked on one another. Jesse slowly moved his right hand to his belly, placing four fingers on the right grip of his six-shooter, the thumb on the left, and withdrew the weapon. He half-cocked the hammer, releasing the cylinder. With his left palm, he spun the half-dozen cartridges chambered inside. They clicked past the pistol's firing pins like a diamondback rattler.

"One good reason, huh?" whispered Jesse. With blurring speed, Jesse snapped his right hand forward, spinning his Colt a half-dozen revolutions before bringing to an instant stop, fully cocked and ready to fire. Kincade saw fury in Jesse's eyes. "There's your one good reason.

"And now I gotta question for you, Kincade. Are you done tryin' to run me out of your life?"

"Yeah," Kincade said.

"Good. 'Cause tomorrow is as good a day to die as any."

And with that, Jesse stood from the fire, walked over to his saddle, unfurled a blanket, lay down, and put his hat over his eyes.

25

The five killers stayed close to the river as they rode into Tombstone. For this job, Logan took only his segundos: Chico Fernandez, Bart Ramsey, Lex Everson, and Coryell. These four were the very best of the very worst, without peer when it came to dealing the art of death. Logan knew that Wyatt Earp kept the peace in Tombstone with an iron fist. Riding in with twenty gunhands would draw the marshal's attention, and Logan didn't want a warning of trouble to be sounded. The four men knew that Logan was headed for a showdown with Kincade, but they hadn't yet been told the plan. That didn't bother them; they were used to getting information on a need to know basis.

On the outskirts of Tombstone, miners pitched their tents. Closer to town, folks built shacks. One very small house had a white picket fence out front. It belonged to a twenty-three-year-old widow, whose young husband had been killed two winters earlier in a Tombstone silver mine explosion. Poor when the couple first arrived, even poorer now, the widow eeked out a living by working fourteen hours a day for the slavedrivers in a Chinese laundry. It had taken the widow over a year to save enough money to repair and paint that picket fence.

As Logan's gang rode past, Everson threw his lariat to catch one of the carefully painted fence posts, dallied up, and tore down twelve feet of the poor widow's prized possession. Just for fun. The woman watched silently from the kitchen window as the mounted scum laughed in unison. She began to softly cry.

Logan said nothing. Whatever his boys did to show their rough side was fine with him. Logan occupied himself with the Cosmopolitan Hotel, the top turrets plainly visible in the center of town. The territorial flag flew over the building. "When I'm finished with Josephine, we'll just have to yank that rag down and mop her saloon floor with it," snarled Logan. "Then we'll just mail it off to any lawman who believes anything he's doing amounts to squat."

"Pull up, boys. This'll do," ordered Logan.

As one, they dismounted near a clump of willows next to the stream. "We'll wait here," said Logan. "Decide how best to burn this burg and barbeque Kincade's sweet little Josephine."

By nightfall the segundos were sitting around the fire, waiting for Logan to speak.

"Fernandez, you're to go into town tomorrow and get the lay of the land. Right now ya look like ya do in them wanted posters. Cut off that mustache and keep your head down. Leave that Mexican sombrero behind and wear Ramsey's Stetson."

Ramsey looked at Chico as if he would kill him if the hat came back damaged.

Logan continued. "Talk to people and see if Kincade's been seen around town. Don't call him by name, you dumb fool, just say a big stranger with lots of guns. Go to the livery and ask if they've stabled a palomino stallion. Go to the blacksmith, 'cause he'll be aware of any new horses in town.

Go to the gunsmith and the general store'n see if any stranger bought ammunition lately. You got my drift?"

"Yeah, yeah, yeah. I ain't stupid."

"I'm not so sure about that. Then check out the saloon in the corner of that hotel on Allen Street. It'll be run by a woman named Josephine."

Fernandez laughed. "Burned her out once on the Cherokee. Burned her out a second time in Benson. Third time's a charm, right boss?"

"'Cept this time, Kincade'll be here. She's his woman, and our bait. I want the layout of the saloon: where the doors are, the bar, the tables, the people that go there. Everything. You got it?"

"Might take me more'n a day."

"Just don't come back without an answer for every question I've asked ya."

"How come he's the lucky one?" Ramsey asked. "What are we supposed to do? Sit here on our butts while he's in a town with doves, and liquor, and gamblin'?"

Logan looked daggers at Ramsey. "No, you sit here on your butts and thank your lucky stars that I ain't killed you yet." With that comforting thought in mind, the five headed for their saddle blankets and a restless night.

26

The Cosmopolitan Hotel was the finest building in Tombstone—bar none. It had been built thanks to Albert Bilicke, a millionaire who had made his fortune in gold mining, but preferred to live in bustling San Francisco with his wife of many years, their five children, twenty grandchildren, and he had forgotten how many great-grandchildren. They were the upper crust of the port city, and haughtily proud of it.

Bilicke's business empire required that he travel frequently. During his stopovers in a town called Benson, he watched the success of Josephine and her Proud Cat Dance Hall and Saloon. He visited with her customers, asking their opinions of her, and why they chose the Proud Cat over the other saloons of Benson. Smart businessman that he was, Bilicke could smell money. He offered Josephine her own place inside the Cosmopolitan, and half ownership of the hotel as well. She refused and refused again. Until the Proud Cat burned.

Josephine was grateful to have a place of refuge, but she laid down some terms as well. No expense was to be spared in the construction, décor, and hiring practices of her new venture. Josephine had an uncanny knack for good business. Bilicke had seen her considerable skills in Benson, so it didn't surprise him when she also turned her attention to the Cosmopolitan Hotel, which, in her estimation, needed to be upgraded to befit the recent change in management.

The Cosmo was located only three blocks from the train depot and soon became a natural gathering place for the community as well as accommodations for travelers. The hotel's front desk was staffed by gentlemen who genuinely welcomed everyone who entered. Thickly upholstered lobby chairs beckoned weary travelers and congenial citizens. Tiffany lamps on tabletops were laced with tassels and crystal. On winter nights, a crackling fire burned in the large fireplace at the head of the lobby. The upstairs rooms were elegantly but conservatively furnished. Every afternoon at four Josephine herself served tea and cakes in a dainty parlor to the women of the town. In exchange they granted her respectability and even admiration.

For the men of Tombstone a different room beckoned entirely. The adjoining saloon she named for herself—the Josephine. It was not just a place to drink, gamble, and enjoy the company of women, it was a luxurious palace. Entrance could be gained either through batwing doors on the street or up a short flight of stairs from the lobby of the Cosmopolitan. The high ceiling was covered in ornate tin. The bar stretched nearly the length of the saloon, with a large mirror decorated with elaborate frostwork. The oak tables were in a variety of sizes, and all the chairs had cushions of various-colored plush. The gambling tables were new and the latest models. Josephine hired only the most experienced dealers, and she kept a constant eye on them to see that each game was unfailingly honest.

At the back of the saloon, several doors led to rooms for

entertainment of an intimate nature, with subdued lighting and soft featherbeds. Josephine's ladies, as she preferred them to be called, were each beautiful in their own distinct way—blondes, brunettes, redheads, whites, blacks, and Orientals. It was Josephine's pleasure to give each her own right to shine, in demeanor and in dress. Each wore her hair in the style most becoming—some with curls piled on top of their heads, some with tresses falling loose onto their shoulders, some with a crown of braids held in place with ivory needles. Their costumes also were individual. They could be formfitting satin and silk corsets with swishing taffeta skirts below. The Oriental girl liked to wear a Japanese kimono, and a lusty brunette sometimes decked herself out in bright leather chaps over her legs exposed in black silk stockings. Josephine helped them design their costumes to be sure they were always in good taste. Then she put the cost of having them made on her expense account.

Josephine demanded that her girls be treated with absolute respect. As had been the rule at the Proud Cat, any wrangler who got out of line was brutally thrown through the batwings by a Samson of a man who only needed a nod from Josephine to do his job. Josie knew from experience that the crowds loved music, so in the fashion of the Proud Cat, a stage was an important feature. The honky-tonk piano player could sing even louder than the piano on which he hammered.

Josephine's ladies were a dozen beauties, but chosen for their talent in performing as well. And perform they did, oftentimes to the raucous applause of a packed house. At the heart of this very special place was the sweet owner herself. Josephine had never been more beautiful. Her dresses were always black—silk, satin, brocade, velvet, lace—always black. They could have beads and bangles, tassels and trimmings, tucks and pleats—always black. Her accessories were always white—a lace shawl festooned over her arms, a white rose tucked in her cleavage, pearls in a long chain or in rows at her throat, little ermine pelts around her shoulders—always white. With her golden hair and crème-colored skin, the word stunning seemed inadequate. But more—much more—than her incredible loveliness was her courtesy, good cheer, and dazzling smile for all who entered. The patrons of the Josephine were falling in love with its proprietress just as her previous patrons had done in Benson.

She could make a nervous eighteen-year-old wrangler feel at ease. "Hello, cowboy. Welcome to the Josephine. I'm Josie in the flesh. May I get you something? The first one's on the house to toast your arrival in Tombstone."

To an old sourdough who was down on his luck she would say, "This one's on me, partner. As much as you've spent in the Josephine, it would be my pleasure."

Chico Fernandez took in all of this information and sealed it in his mind to relate to Logan. He had done what he was told—talked with folks at the livery stable, the blacksmith shop, the general store. There was no sign of Kincade yet. Chico's favorite haunt was the saloon, but in less than two days he had spent all his money and could hardly hang out there any longer without a drink or a game of poker. So he took up a position in an alley near the smithy. From that inconspicuous point he spied on the men who entered the Josephine, counting how many were townsmen and how many were cowboys or drifters. No one resembled Kincade. He rolled his smoke and thought of returning to Logan that evening. He would never make it. Not that evening. Not ever.

27

Big Red had been a blacksmith as a boy in Ireland. He kept on with his trade when he and his younger sister Abby immigrated to Sandia, New Mexico. They were happy living in a small house adjacent to the smithy, and Abby was being courted by a young farmer who was also from Ireland.

One day a mean-looking gang rode into town and hired Big Red to shoe their horses, which he did. When he asked for payment, one of them hit him from behind with a metal bar and knocked him cold. They raped and beat up Abby, and in a few days she died of her wounds. They torched the house and smithy. That's when Big Red came to Tombstone.

Big Red was a giant of a man. Six and a good half feet of steel, covered by a thin veneer of flesh and blood. His two arms looked like railroad ties, his neck the width of a tree trunk. All topped off with a wild tangle of hair the color of strawberries. Red was a man of few words—a true force to be reckoned with. Working alone, with white-hot iron his whole life, does that to a fellow.

He liked Tombstone. Work was good. He had friends. But Red's affection for animals and kids was surpassed only by his hidden love for Josephine.

Oh, he would never, could never, say anything to her about it. He just didn't have the nerve. Even in the few short months she had been in town, Big Red knew that most of Tombstone had grown to love Josephine, just as he had. And oftentimes, he was ashamed that his affection for her might have included a look or two at her stunning figure, rather than the sweetness and compassion of her soul.

Big Red would do anything to protect Josephine, and for two days he had been sure she needed protection. A burly Mexican had been questioning people all over town. He asked about a lot of things, but seemed particularly interested in the Josephine: What time did it open? What time did it shut down? Was there a side door or a rear door? How many men worked there?

And he asked about the proprietress herself: What time did she show up? Did she come to work every day? Was she ever seen with a tall stranger who wore a lot of guns? Since Sandia, Big Red could smell an outlaw a mile off, and this fellow was putting up quite a stench.

All along, Big Red had thought the man looked familiar. Then when he came to question the blacksmith about any strange horses in town, it struck him like a thunderbolt. The Mexican was one of the gang that had ruined his life in Sandia. The hombre had shaved off his mustache, but Red would recognize those bushy eyebrows and mean, little lizard eyes anywhere. Evil was always in the eyes. Red knew, without question, that this trash was planning do in Tombstone what he had done in Sandia. The Josephine would be raided and burned, and his beloved Josephine would suffer as his sister Abby had. Big Red could not let that happen.

The evening of the second day this hombre had been standing for an hour and a half in an alleyway, watching the batwing doors of the Josephine. Red could stand it no longer. He was angry. Very angry.

Red's forge had been turning iron into putty all that day in a way so effective that putty had turned into a thin, white hot soup. Big Red took one of his casting bowls and filled it to the brim with molten metal. His massive hands gripped a three-foot-long pair of tongs, strangling the bowl, which had begun to glow from the searing heat. He turned from his forge, walked into the alley, and moved toward the dark man. Funny how such a huge person could naturally move with the grace of a cat.

The outlaw smelled the liquid, and felt the heat, long before he realized that Big Red was right behind him. Fernandez spun on his heels, snapping up a Winchester from his right leg. But it never got any farther than that. Red knocked off Fernandez' hat, held the molten bowl over the killer's head, and poured it over his skull. Every single last scalding drop.

Big Red was used to the smell of burning hair and flesh. It was a natural part of his business. Didn't bother him at all. Neither did the smell of a very bad man, whose entire head was stripped of hair and flesh in less than six seconds.

As Chico Fernandez crashed to the ground, Big Red looked into the empty bone sockets of a grinning skull. That'll learn ya to harm Abby and Miss Josephine, thought Red.

That same afternoon, the four men at Logan's camp paced, circled, and snapped at each other. Filled with pent-up anger and impatience, they were like steam engine boilers ready to blow.

"Where the hell is Fernandez?" Logan snarled.

"Damn Mex!" spit Everson. "He's probably shacked up with some cheap whore."

"We hang around here much longer, rust'll start flakin' off me," complained Coryell.

"Yeah, let's go. Damn Chico's got my hat," complained Ramsey. "Let's skin our smoke wagons and get to work."

"Okay. You three get into town tonight and keep hidden. Don't let nobody see your faces. Find Chico. Coryell, you find some high ground and set up across from Josephine's saloon. Keep your eyes open for Kincade. I'm certain he's comin', if he ain't here already. You see somethin', you get yourselves back here pronto.

"Then we'll all ride in together and tear Kincade apart."

28

Late afternoon that same day, Kincade and Jesse could make out the rise to the south that held the town of Tombstone. About two miles out, they saw the spires of the Cosmopolitan Hotel. Kincade knew that Josie was beneath those spires, preparing for the evening's festivities. As in any mining town throughout the frontier, Saturday night was the favorite. And Josephine reserved her very finest, from her ladies to her libations, for Saturday nights. Inside the Josephine, the proprietress always thrilled her guests with the dazzling gowns she wore only on Saturday nights. This Saturday night would be like no other, though not for reasons Josephine was aware of.

Below the rise of the cemetery on Boot Hill, not a half-mile from where Logan and his men planned the destruction of the saloon and its mistress, Kincade and Jesse dismounted. The big man had been quiet for many hours, and Jesse didn't press him.

But around the campfire, Jesse asked, "What's the play?"

"We know Josephine's life is at stake. Logan will go to her saloon."

Kincade laid out his plan, conceived of, worked on, and reworked again and again since he had pulled Logan's bullet from his left shoulder. Jesse listened intently. It seemed as if the spirits of Whiskey Pete, Little Blue, and Finley all listened to the plotted vengeance as well. The coals from the camp-fire burned low, blood red. Finally Kincade finished and looked toward Jesse. "Got it?"

"Sounds good to me. Later tonight?"

"That's my plan."

Darkness arrived in all its ebony glory. Kincade and Jesse could see the lights from the top floors of the Cosmopolitan Hotel burning brightly. When the wind shifted just right, they could hear the Josephine's honky-tonk piano player pounding away in full force. Kincade and Jesse were more than ready to move. The awareness of Logan triggered memories of the way he had ravaged everyone and every-thing around him. Something made the two men choke. It wasn't the smoke from the night's fire. It was Logan's stench.

Gold Digger heard it first: the crack of dry limbs. The palomino's neck jerked up, his nostrils flaring as the muscles pulled taut. Two riders were approaching the camp.

Jesse spun from his crouch, grabbing the Winchester 73 from Digger's saddle, throwing it into Kincade's waiting hands. With a lightning-fast snap of his wrist, Kincade quickly racked the first cartridge, leveled the barrel to the trees where the two riders were about to appear, and placed his finger on the trigger. His right hand prepared to chamber and fire the full magazine.

Jesse rolled to his right and yanked his .44 from the waist belt. He slammed the hammer back and jammed his elbow into his side where the recoil would be best received. Jesse was ready to fan six into the two riders as soon as they cleared the high brush.

"Show yourselves," Kincade shouted, "or you'll be blown in half."

Another crackle of dried twigs, and the two riders appeared. Another split second, and both Kincade's and Jesse's guns would have been set afire. But as yet they hadn't opened up. Thank God they hadn't.

The two riders dismounted, moved forward, and stepped into the fading firelight. Both riders wore long dusters. The shorter and much thinner held a gentleman's cane. Beneath his topcoat he sported a gambler's vest, adorned with a shoulder holster tucked into the left of his chest. On his right hip sat a cross-draw rig and a left-handed holster, enabling him, should he find it necessary, to pull two guns before the object of his attention could blink.

The taller of the two wore a black hat, the brim and crown perfectly flat. He was big, foreboding, utterly confident in himself, with the air of being in control of whatever situation in which he found himself. The silver badge on his chest caught the firelight. "Hello, Kincade. I got a wire that you'd be showing up in my town."

Kincade stood motionless, the Winchester leveled and aimed squarely at the chest of the larger of the two strangers. "Marshal, if you've come to arrest me, I'm telling you politely to move on. I've got unfinished business here in Tombstone, and I'll not go behind bars until it's settled."

"Wyatt," interrupted the other stranger. "I think your friend here . . . a Mister Kincade, I believe . . . it appears your friend may be wondering what our intentions are, riding into his camp tonight."

Neither Kincade nor Jesse moved.

"Perhaps, Doc, they're wondering if I might have seen his picture on a certain poster with the notation Wanted Dead or Alive, and if perhaps I'm here to do more than simply

welcome him and his sidekick . . . it is Jesse Keller, isn't it?
. . . perhaps they wonder if we're standing here in order to
splatter them all over this yard. Do you suppose that might
be the case, Doc?" And the tall man with the silver badge
over his heart raised his left eyebrow toward his companion.

"I have an idea," said the thinner of the two riders. "Why
don't you tell Mr. Kincade that you know all about what
happened up there in Montana. Assure him that you and I
are both aware of Mr. Wil Logan's double-cross, and that we
have no wish to make a mess of him, of his friend, or of my
best shirt that I retrieved from Mr. Woo's laundry only this
afternoon. What say you, my good friend?"

The tall stranger scrunched up his jaw and rubbed the
chin stubble with his right hand. "You know . . . I believe the
doctor has exactly the correct prescription for the continued
good health of us all." And with that, Wyatt Earp and Doc
Holliday grinned ear to ear.

Kincade's heartbeat slowed, the tension disappeared, and
both hands lowered the Winchester. Marshal Wyatt Earp
strode up to Kincade and extended a handshake. John
Henry "Doc" Holliday tipped his hat to Jesse.

"You know, Wyatt," commented Doc, "I really think you
had best enroll yourself in the School of Southern
Gentlemen, of which I am a graduate summa cum laude. Not
only would you improve your skills when welcoming visitors to
our fine hamlet, but you would save the town tailor from the
tedious task of patching errant bullet holes in your duster."

All four men laughed. Kincade looked at Wyatt Earp.
"That mean I'm no longer wanted dead or alive?"

"The government posters are down. But I know why
you're here. You're wanted dead—and not alive—by the
Logan gang."

"Are they here?" Kincade tensed.

"Probably, but they're keeping a low profile—so far." He faced Kincade. "As a U.S. lawman, Logan is my problem. He's wanted, and I'll take him in."

"He's been my lifelong enemy, Marshal. And now he's after the woman I love. I'd say that makes him *my* problem."

Earp continued. "I'll not have my town shot up unless it's done legal. That's why the good doctor and I rode out to find you. Step over here." The marshal pointed his finger at Jesse and motioned him to stand alongside Kincade.

"Raise your right hands." They did. "Swear to uphold the law." They did. "You're deputized." Wyatt Earp handed each a star.

Doc Holliday spoke. "He tried to make me do that. I told him his salary was unacceptable."

"You can make it your fight if you want to, Kincade. I trust you will uphold the honor of the badge." They went back to their horses. Before they could mount, Doc began coughing so violently that he had to lean against the saddle and grip the horn.

"Doc, you all right?" the marshal asked.

"Like a daisy. Just give me a minute." Holliday took a white handkerchief from his pocket and wiped his mouth. "Okay, let's ride."

"What's wrong with the doc?" Jesse asked as he pinned on his badge.

"Consumption."

"What's that?"

"A disease that's eating the life out of him. Earp watches him like a hawk."

"Seems they're a lot like us—blood brothers."

Kincade smiled. "Forever and ever."

The lights of the Cosmopolitan Hotel beckoned in the

distance. Josephine's enthusiastic honky-tonk piano player entertained the ever-growing crowd. Kincade pinned on his silver star. Things had changed for the two men standing around a dying campfire just below Boot Hill on the outskirts of Tombstone.

Better for them—worse for Wil Logan.

29

Tombstone had a reputation for many things, including silver, cattle, and the Josephine Saloon. The men who handled the first two inevitably congregated at the third.

Across the street from the Cosmopolitan Hotel and several doors down from Red's blacksmith shop sat a large two-story building. Used by the cattle processors, it was . . . plain and simple . . . a slaughterhouse. When the cattle drives hit Tombstone, most of the herds would be loaded onto railway cars and sent off to the dining tables of the East. But a hundred or so head from every herd would be moved to Tombstone's own slaughterhouse. The bellowing livestock didn't take a bullet between the eyes solely for their meat. The butchers needed the hides for leather—for saddles and holsters and gunbelts and harnesses and such.

First the cattle were herded into the front of the building. After the doomed animals had departed this world, the butchers stripped the meat. The bones and carcasses were then dragged into the next room. That room was filled with what looked like open stone coffins. But these were larger than those found in any Boot Hill. They were three times as large. Stone vaults, with no lids. Side by side, row by row. About thirty of them.

Inside these vaults bubbled highly toxic acid.

The slaughterhouse crew would drag the cattle carcasses to the vaults. Using hooks much larger than a rancher would use for snagging hay bales, they would heave each carcass up and over the side walls and into the vault . . . two or three in each. As soon as the remains of the animal hit the acid, the butchers would jump back like jackrabbits as a tremendous boil frothed up, mightier than any witch's caldron. The blistering acid tore at what remained of the beast, stripping it of all hair, all bone, all flesh. All that would be left was the leather hide. All in all, it was a very efficient process, start to finish.

Tombstone lived by few rules. But the town slaughterhouse had one: Don't ever let that acid splash on you when heaving a carcass in or out. Several of the crew had forgotten those words of warning over the years, and their scarred faces and bodies bore grotesque marks of eaten flesh, much worse than any fire could ever produce.

Logan's three men had been stalking the dim streets of Tombstone with no luck. "Where the hell is Fernandez?" snarled Coryell. "He'd better not be pickin' over Josephine. If Kincade's in town, that would muck up our party way too early."

"Where the hell is that Mexican?" said Ramsey. "We're supposed to keep hidden, and I can't see a damn thing."

"Maybe we can get a view of who's comin' and goin' to the Josephine from that building," Everson said. The three reached the back entrance of Tombstone's slaughterhouse.

"What the hell is that stink?" asked Everson as Ramsey kicked open the alley door of the two-story building. "Maybe we'll get a good view of the saloon, but God, this place stinks worse than a skunk."

"Shut up," barked Ramsey. "You just do as you're told. We're here to look, not smell. We'll spot Chico and yank him back to face Logan. He'll be dog meat when the boss is done."

"Somethin's dead in here," said Everson. "Over and over dead." But the three were used to the stench of death, so they pushed forward.

Moving through the front room and into the darkness of the second, the three bandits saw light filtering through the windows that faced the Josephine. The glass was about ten feet up the wall. But no matter. They knew they would have a clear look from up there. All they needed to do was stand on the edge of one of those large stone boxes, all lined up side by side. Their minds raced with anticipation. What if Kincade was standing out front? To hell with Chico Fernandez! Letting Logan know they had seen Kincade would sit real good . . . maybe even earn them a turn or two at Josephine herself.

"Let's get up there," said Coryell. Ramsey ran forward, leaping on the first vault, immediately followed by Coryell and Everson.

"Nothing can stop us," Ramsey boasted as they leaped upward, "absolutely nothing."

Except for one thing.

An experienced butcher would know and never forget that years and years of splashing cattle blood and guts leaves more than a very unpleasant smell. It leaves a viscous scum that is slicker than horse snot. A butcher would know. An outlaw would not.

Coryell, Everson, and Ramsey found out just how slick that scum was the moment their boots hit the vault's edge. Unfortunately, the three were unable to share their surprise among themselves. All three plunged headlong into the vat's liquid, disappearing from sight in a thrashing explosion of unspeakable agony, and utter efficiency.

The hides retrieved from the first stone vault the next day would not be used for saddles or holsters or harnesses.

Wil Logan didn't know it yet, but he would be entering Tombstone alone, without gunfighters to back him up or information about Kincade.

It didn't matter. Because he had an ace up his sleeve that would insure Kincade's death.

30

Jesse and Kincade stood at the hitching rail across the street from the windows of the Josephine. Inside, they could see the crowd. Cowboys lined up one by one, preferring to stand and belly up to the bar. Hoisting their boots to the brass rail at their feet, they would proudly place both hands splayed on the polished wood, rapping their glasses smartly to catch the attention of the barkeeps, and any ladies who might be gazing their way. "Whiskey!" they would shout, and the bartenders would eagerly respond, splashing their glasses full. Once in hand, the cowboys would spin around to the crowd, enabling them to take stock of the ladies like proud roosters counting their hens.

If they had had a lick of sense, their eyes would have bypassed all the powder, plumage, and the promise of petticoats. If they had known, those cowboys would have quickly placed their glasses, empty or full, on the bar, tipped their hats to the bartenders, and bid them goodnight, preferring to live another day rather than get drunk another night. For there, inside the Josephine Saloon, sitting about twelve feet from the piano player's stage, waited Wil Logan.

Kincade and Jesse had two choices. They could either

enter the Josephine through the Allen Street entrance, or come in from behind via the interior of the Cosmopolitan's lobby. They chose both. Jesse took the hotel lobby entrance. Kincade chose the batwings. The two of them looked at one another as they left the darkness that surrounded the hitching post, and began their move toward the lights of the hotel. They said nothing. What would be the point? From the innocence of childhood days, to a lifetime of learning what it meant to care or to kill, it had all led to this: a warm Saturday night in a lawless town named after the stone tablets of dead men.

How appropriate, Kincade thought to himself. How could the reckoning possibly take place anywhere but here? Kincade watched Jesse step onto the wooden planking of the boardwalk, pull back the door to the Cosmopolitan's lobby, and disappear inside. Well, this is it.

Kincade paused in front of the batwings facing Allen Street. He looked up at the lights of the hotel. Room after room of bright lights. He wondered how many couples were up there at that moment, Dancing in the rooms of the Cosmopolitan. The building almost looked like a carnival. Red brick, with each of the rooms' street-front exteriors decorated with a painted white arch, like a monotone rainbow sitting atop each window.

Kincade slowly turned back to Allen Street. He looked west, to the shops of Tombstone. Then north at the dark windows of the slaughterhouse. And to the east, where the train depot sat, quiet for the night. At the hitching rail, Gold Digger waited. Yes, I'll try to be careful, my old friend, thought Kincade. But Josephine is here. And no harm will ever come to her again, not so long as I draw breath.

Kincade pushed the batwings of the Josephine left and right and stepped inside.

The sight of her took his breath away. His dreams of her were not nearly so lovely. Josephine wore a black silk dress with layers of ruffles cascading from waist to hem. A wide lace collar was held by an ivory cameo at her incredible cleavage. There were white flowers in her golden hair.

Kincade stood just to the inside of the batwings, his heart pounding. No matter what he had been, no matter how many years he had spent living alone, Josephine had forever changed him.

Kincade now understood the trails of his life . . . the ultimate reason he had been sold by the old Indian, the reason he had learned how to care about Jesse Keller, the reason he would stop the scum-sucking gutter trash named Logan. Every bit of his life, the good and the bad, had forged Kincade into the man he had become, and for some unexplainable reason, this man had captured Josephine's heart, and she his. If he were to be killed tonight, it would all have been worth it. Because of Josephine, and for the first time in his life, Kincade felt complete.

As she always did when she heard the batwings swing open, Josephine turned, eager to welcome her newest guest. Her jaw fell open . . . "It can't be!"

And at the very same moment Josephine's eyes met Kincade's, Wil Logan saw the gunfighter he had waited years to kill.

He saw Kincade . . .

31

In booming bravado, Logan shouted, "Kincade, it's finally just you and me!" He stood and reached for his guns.

It would take a moment, but only a moment, for the patrons of the Josephine to realize what was about to happen. Only a moment for the honky-tonk piano player who was in the midst of a festive tune, for the attentive bartenders busily pouring generous drinks for the thirsty cowboys of Tombstone, for those standing and those seated at tables, it only took a moment to realize what was happening. Their wish for a fine Saturday night in the town of Tombstone was cataclysmically coming apart, destroyed by the angel of death himself: Wil Logan.

Kincade had been momentarily distracted by seeing Josephine after so long a time. But Logan had no such hesitation. He immediately overturned the table before him, launching it across the room toward Kincade and the entrance to the Josephine. The bottle on the table crashed forward, throwing shattered glass onto frightened guests left and right. Logan then heaved three chairs, two of which slammed into the piano player who fell to the floor. The goldfish jar full of tips, just above the piano's high note keys, tipped over, spilling the change onto the hardwood floor below. A big ranch hand who had been thoroughly enjoying the piano player's tune . . . so much so that he had tipped back his chair onto two hind legs . . . was upended and smashed backward into yet another table. He found himself flat on his back wondering what the hell had happened, and just which no-good coot he would have to beat the tar out of to make sure it never happened again. But he would never get that chance. No cowboy had ever run into a cold-blooded murderer as ruthless as Wil Logan.

The saloon erupted in chaos. In hysteric haste, chairs were overturned, drinks spilled, cards scattered. Gamblers scooped their winnings into their hats and bolted out the batwing doors. Other men ducked under tables or plastered themselves against walls that seemed out of the path of the gunfighters. Josephine's ladies were screaming and shoving, struggling to get up the stairs and out of the room.

Seeing the blue steel of Logan's six-guns clear leather, Kincade knew there would be two-foot flames of gunfire belching from both barrels before he could take another breath. He skinned both his Colts and dropped to the floor, rolling and firing at the enraged bull facing him with guns blazing. Kincade quickly returned to his feet and lunged toward the bar. His head and back smashed into the wood just above the bar's brass foot railing. He was dazed, but he wasn't hit.

Shaking his head to clear it, he grabbed a chair by the leg and heaved it toward the advancing Logan. As it sailed across the room, Kincade jumped up and emptied both chambers. Logan laughed maniacally as he staggered but did not fall. He threw a heavy glass liquor bottle at the bar, which exploded just over Kincade's head.

Josephine stood dumbstruck. She couldn't believe the

mayhem around her. Her head flinched as she focused on
Logan, suddenly recognizing him as the man who had
burned her place to the ground not once but twice.
Josephine flashed back to the horrors on the Cherokee—
the station in flames, the blood, the killing. And the Proud
Cat, recoiling at the appalling memory of Finley burning
alive in the fire. No, not again! her mind screamed out. How
is this possible? How can this all be happening? After all
these years, all the miles, all the sleepless nights filled with
unspeakable nightmares . . . how can this be happening
here? In Tombstone . . . to my guests . . . my place . . . not now,
not here, not again! But hell had returned. She couldn't just
stand there doing nothing.

As Kincade was dodging and ducking Logan's barrage
of lead, he suddenly became aware of Josephine. He was
horrified. Surely she would be cut to ribbons as she darted
between him and Logan, consumed with the safety of her
ladies and her guests. She seemed to pay no attention to the
hail of bullets flying around her.

"Josie, for God's sake, turn over that table and get behind
it. He'd just as soon kill you as me." She quickly did as he
said, knowing she would only put Kincade in greater danger
if he felt he had to protect her.

Kincade sailed across two tables, knocking one down to
the hardwood floor, spinning around as he wedged his back
to the table's upturned top. With blazing speed, he opened
the cylinders from both revolvers, dumping the spent casings,
and reloading twelve from his chest bandoleer.

At exactly the same moment, the back door to the Josephine
crashed open, and Jesse burst onto the stair landing. He
slammed into two screaming ladies trying to escape. As the
three of them tussled, Jesse's eyes searched the room for his

blood brother below. No matter what happened to him in the next few moments, Jesse was determined that Kincade must not die. Absolutely must not!

Jesse saw Logan move forward toward an overturned table, kicking a chair backward so violently that it disintegrated against the rear wall on impact. Logan had his guns jammed backward to waist level, each thumb shoved onto the hammers, eyes wild, voice roaring like an animal. Jesse had to do something. He had to get Logan's attention, now!

Jesse fired his gun three times and shouted over the wailing and screaming, "Logan! Your boy Jesse's back! I come to kill ya!"

Josephine immediately recognized Jesse from the stories Kincade had shared with her in Benson. She screamed, "Help him, Jesse! For God's sake, help him!"

Jesse cleared the three steps in one gigantic leap and somersaulted onto the saloon floor below. His gun was cocked and aimed toward the dog that had tormented so many for so long. But Logan was fast—fast enough to spin on his heels. At the very moment Jesse was pulling the trigger, Logan emptied his guns into Jesse; blood spurted from his stomach like a ruptured dam. His only shot went into the ceiling.

Kincade was so intent on reloading that he was hardly aware of other actions in the room. Grabbing the leg of a stool, Kincade heaved it over the top of the table. As it sailed across the room, Kincade jumped up to continue his fire. But he couldn't. He could only watch Jesse as he desperately attempted to distract Logan in order to save Kincade's life. He heard the shots, saw Jesse double over and slump onto the floor at Logan's feet. "Oh, God, no . . ." Kincade exploded with nearly uncontrollable anger, his pistols opening up on Logan.

Josephine screamed. "JESS!"

As Kincade's first shots left the barrels, Logan sprang toward the saloon's front bar like a cat. Kincade's bullets flew by Logan's head, slamming one after the other into the piano, blowing out the back side.

Logan was up and over the bar, vaulting past the petrified bartender whose terrified eyes darted between the madman and the gunnysack Logan had stuffed beneath the bar when he first arrived in the Josephine. Logan glared at the bartender as he crashed down into the walkway below the back bar's mirror. "One move, and I'll blow your head off."

Suddenly, the room went quiet. Only a few whimpers from customers who were now experiencing their first bitter taste and acrid smell of what hell was really like.

"Jess . . . Jess. Are you alright?" yelled Kincade.

Nothing.

"JESSE!" . . .

32

"Kincade . . . he's not moving! Jesse's not moving!" screamed Josephine.

"Stay there. Get down. Don't move, Josie," answered Kincade. "Please . . . don't move." One of Josephine's saloon ladies, crouched behind the table with her, began to cry.

Like the viper he was, Logan began to laugh from behind the bar. "Welcome to my party, Kincade. Ain't this fun? After all these years, it's just you and me provin' who's the better man."

"Then step out, you scum-sucking pig," Kincade came back.

Dragging the gunnysack to his side, Logan laughed again—a quiet, sinister cackle of a laugh. "You're a sad case, Kincade. Ever since I knowed you, all you cared about was your sense of respect. Remember the woman passenger at Corinne? Tried to save her, didn't ya? Now, you got your pretty little Josephine caught in a cross fire. Hell, you can't even take care of your women. You, and your kind, make me sick." Again, Logan laughed through the foam spilling from the corners of his mouth.

"I said step out, Logan," yelled Kincade. "Step out and get yours."

"I told you, Kincade. It's my party. Why, you're my guest of honor. I even brought a little present for you. Cutest little present you ever did see." Again, Logan laughed, and again, the cry. But it wasn't from Josephine's saloon lady. The cry was coming from behind and below the bar.

"You been a pain in my butt all my life. But, seein's this is my party, and you bein' my guest of honor, I'll give you your present anyway."

Kincade's hands tightened on the pearl grips of the twin Colts.

"You bein' such a gentleman and all, I think I'll just stand up, and give it to you personally," announced Logan.

"Go ahead, you tub 'a guts," said Kincade.

"Are you ready?"

Kincade yanked back the hammers on both guns, ready to split Logan's head into a canoe. "Sure, Wil. I'm ready."

"That's good, Kincade. I've been waiting to give this to you for some time." And with that, Kincade could hear Logan, with some scuffled effort, stand. Without wasting a second, Kincade aimed his six-shooters toward the back bar and Logan's voice.

Kincade's entire body froze.

There, in front of Wil Logan and pinned by the throat, wild eyed and absolutely terrified, stood the six-year-old girl from Julesburg:

Melissa Wilcox.

33

Little Melissa was so afraid.

Feeling Logan's callused hand choking off nearly all her air; smelling his wretched breath swirling into her nostrils; coughing from the acrid gunsmoke that wafted through the air; staring into the barrels of Kincade's guns; looking at the shattered tables and chairs; watching the stunned piano man and paralyzed bartender gape at her with eyes the size of saucers; seeing the terror in the horror-struck faces of everyone who now stood frozen in their tracks throughout the room; seeing a man lying on the floor covered in blood; little Melissa Wilcox knew she was going to die just like her mama.

"Don't shoot me, mister. Please don't shoot me!" Her tiny voice was between a scream and a sob. Kincade could plainly see the shivering terror ripple through the little girl's fragile body.

Logan had planned for this exact moment since he had mentally turned the schoolyard in Silver Spike into a shooting gallery. Seeing Melissa in Julesburg, then following her, grabbing her at the creek—it was all so perfect. Melissa's kidnapping had nothing to do with providing nightly amusement for the gang who rode with him, but as insurance for exactly this moment. It was why Logan held his dogs back, warning that if any of them so much as touched the girl, he would rip their arms off.

Logan wanted the little girl fresh, unharmed, unspoiled, assuring him that when he finally met Kincade face to face, the little girl would stop Kincade from doing anything to Logan for fear of harming the child.

After Melissa's abduction, Logan turned the girl over to one of his segundos, Lex Everson, who was to keep her captive until the time was right. Understanding Everson's pace with the little girl would be different from theirs, he gave Everson orders to meet the gang in Tombstone, and promised the outlaw he would slit his throat if anything happened to her.

Logan reveled in the outcome of his planning. He always schemed for an ace in the hole. Knowing Kincade since childhood, little Melissa was Logan's ace of hearts.

Kincade hesitated, riveted by the panic in Melissa's eyes. "Don't."

Again, Logan laughed, a sickening, wretched, evil laugh. His assumptions were fulfilled.

"Do you like it?" hissed Logan.

"Let her go, Logan," said Kincade.

"That's just what you said at Corinne. Remember what I did to that lady?" Logan took his gun hand, and slowly moved the barrel of his six-shooter to little Melissa's temple. "Who's gonna shoot first, Kincade? You? I see you're wearin' a deputy badge, and here I am wanted dead or alive. Why not shoot me now, Kincade? Of course I might just dodge a bit, and you'd hit Melissa here. Too bad your heart's so soft."

Logan glared at Kincade with revulsion. "Hey, Kincade, now that you're a law dog, I think it'd be best if you took off that star and tossed it over to me."

Kincade didn't move.

"I said toss it over!" Logan rammed the barrel of his pistol into Melissa's head, hard. He cocked the hammer. The small girl let out a terrified wail.

Josephine screamed, "Oh no, please. She's just a little girl! NO!"

Slowly, Kincade holstered one gun and unpinned the deputy badge, tossing it toward Logan.

"You see, I might get some criticism for shooting an officer of the law, but not for shooting a man wanted dead or alive for a little murder and robbery in Corinne." His laugh was almost a growl. "I seen those posters with your picture. Shooting you will not only give me pleasure but a reward from the Wells Fargo folks. Now what could be nicer?"

Logan was in his element. "Well, I think I'll end this guessing game and fire the first shot myself. Or is it your turn? I forget. Up to me—up to you—who's gonna die, Kincade?"

34

The rage inside Kincade rose up like a tidal wave. Bigger, larger, more ferocious than anything he had ever imagined possible. But Logan was right. From this angle, Kincade's shot could kill the little girl.

Logan's finger tightened on the trigger, as his reptilian eyes locked onto the paralyzed gunfighter. "You've always been the one, haven't you, Kincade? You and your self-righteous ways. You were weak when we was kids. You're even weaker today. Let's see how brave you are at dyin' . . ."

Logan's final bravado was all the distraction Jesse Keller needed. Clutching his bloody shirt in his left hand, and a gun that held one final bullet in his right, Jesse pulled himself to his feet and lurched toward Logan.

Using the speed reserved solely for a very few brave men, Jesse put his final round into the brain of one Wil Logan. The shot was so clean, and so close, that it blew the far side of Logan's skull into a hundred pieces. The flared lead exited Logan's shattered head and slammed into the wooden face of the bar in the Josephine Saloon.

Josephine rushed to catch Melissa as she crumpled to the floor. "Someone go get the doctor! Hurry!"

As Kincade ran to break the fall of Jesse, Wyatt Earp and Doc Holliday crashed through the hotel lobby door, six-guns at the ready, entering the saloon itself. They ran to Kincade and knelt by his side. Seeing the ghastly wound in Jesse's gut, it was clear to both of them that Jess was at death's doorstep. Both felt unbelievably hollow for being only minutes late. But now, there was nothing they or anyone else could do.

Kincade held Jesse in his arms, wishing he could do something . . . anything. Jesse's question came as a whisper. "Is she . . . is the little girl . . . okay?" asked Jesse in a voice that could barely be heard.

"Yes. She's okay . . . thanks to you."

"Are you hit?" asked Jesse.

Kincade shook his head. "Be still. The doctor's coming . . ."

Jesse's voice was soft, and he clutched his stomach, which was pumping blood onto the saloon floor. "Kincade, I gotta tell you something . . ."

"You don't need to tell me anything. Just take it easy till the doctor comes."

"Listen . . ." Jesse's glazing eyes lowered to the old Indian medicine bag, resting on Kincade's chest.

"Please . . . just listen . . ."

35

Kincade cradled Jesse. He bent closer so he could understand his soft, slow words.

"You remember when I was a kid there was this lady named Miz Agnes Johnson? She took me in."

"Yes, Jess. I remember Agnes Johnson."

"And I told you how upset she was when I said I was gonna join Logan's gang?"

Kincade nodded.

"And remember I said she'd told me somethin' about Logan that was too awful for me to believe?" Jesse looked into Kincade's eyes. "There's got to be a right time to tell somethin'— 'specially if it's important. Now's the right time to tell you somethin' 'cause it's all the time I got."

"Jess," Kincade said. "I really don't . . ."

Jesse grasped Kincade's hand hard. "Please . . ." Kincade fell silent.

"Miz Agnes Johnson had a sister named Angela . . . married a soldier from the fort outside 'a town. He treated her like dirt. Even so, she birthed him two boys at one beddin'.

"The two babies looked so much alike that the soldier couldn't tell 'em apart. So, he took a knife and carved two

different marks on their arms. Angela hated him for doin'
it, but he told her to shut up. He wasn't one to take orders
from nobody, 'cept the two cavalry officers that he named
the boys after.

"Agnes Johnson said these two boys was as different as
night and day. One was good. The other was bad. Worse than
bad. He'd drown newborn kittens, set fire to their neighbor's
shed, things like that. Older he got, the worse it got. His ma
would say to her soldier husband, 'That's your son—not
mine! He's just like you!' He beat her bad for that."

Wyatt Earp and Doc Holliday stood above Jesse, listening
to every word.

"One day, these twins was playin' in the yard. 'Bout half a
dozen renegade Indians snuck up and grabbed the two
boys. The captain at the fort said when too many girl babies
had been born in a tribe, the braves would steal white boys
and bring 'em up as Indians."

Jesse's voice was getting softer, and Kincade had to lean
closer to hear him.

"Angela went crazy. Her husband and a troop of soldiers
went lookin' for the Indians that'd took those boys. Found
'em too. But one of the twins was gone. Seemed one boy had
been stolen by an old Indian who'd never had a son.
Disappeared with him."

The Tombstone doctor arrived. He opened his satchel.
Holliday took a knife and helped to cut away Jesse's shirt,
exposing a horrific wound. He held back the cloth as the
doctor did his best to stop the increasing flow of blood. Jesse
kept talking.

"The boy they found was the bad one. They could tell right
away from the mark carved into his arm." Jesse clenched his
teeth in excruciating pain. But Kincade listened, knowing
that for some reason, Jesse felt he had to finish.

"Miz Agnes Johnson's sister never got over losin' the one boy she loved. She'd cry all night sometimes. She hated the son they found. Whenever the boy would make hell, she'd say to him, 'Your brother would never do something like that. If I had to lose one son, why couldn't it have been you?' I was there. I heard her say it."

As the town doctor tried his best, Holliday pressed his hand against Jesse's gut, failing to stem the loss of blood. Jess was approaching delirium.

"This boy . . . the one they found . . . he grew up hating his brother. His ma finally died of a broken heart. The boy blamed his brother for that too." Jesse stopped, his eyes began to flutter. The doctor put his stethoscope back in his bag and slowly shook his head to Holliday and Earp. Josephine gasped, holding Melissa Wilcox close to her heart.

Jesse began to breathe in short rapid bursts. With one very weak hand, Jess pointed a trembling finger to the Indian medicine bag on Kincade's chest, where the skin began to crawl.

"Kincade . . ." Jesse whispered. "Go look at Wil's arm. Miz Agnes Johnson . . . her sister Angela was your mother."

As Jesse labored for breath, Wyatt walked the few paces to where Wil Logan's body lay. The marshal took the fabric on the sleeve of Logan's right arm in his powerful hands, tore and tore again; then he stood up, and stepped back.

There, carved into Wil Logan's dead flesh, were five gashes. The first four resembled a lightning bolt. The fifth single line stood by itself. But those first four lines weren't a depiction of a message from the heavens. The four linked together to form a "W," a message from hell.

The scar on Kincade's right bicep began to ache, as the old Indian's secret of the medicine bag and leather patch inside were revealed. The "K" stood for Kincade. But the final line wasn't a line at all. It was an "L." It stood, on the arms of both men, for the last named they shared: Logan.

Wil was Kincade's Blood.

36

Friends, really good friends, know instinctively, without talking about it, what makes the other so special. Jesse and Kincade had known each other for nearly all their lives. Over the years, they had become almost like brothers. That brotherhood had been built on caring enough to understand each other's strengths and weaknesses, while judging neither. Their friendship was built on trust, respect, a love for life, and a belief in one another. They were brothers in their hearts.

The brotherhood in their eyes was evident to everyone as Kincade and Jesse looked at one another for the last time, on the floor of the corner saloon of the Cosmopolitan Hotel in Tombstone, Arizona Territory. In the final analysis, it's all in the eyes.

Kincade felt Jesse's grip tighten in his hand. But only for a moment. A moment was all it took.

Jesse died in Kincade's arms.

Tombstone's Boot Hill was a cold and lonely place, fit for no one but the dead. The peal of the one church bell only made that bleak Sunday morning all the lonelier, as Kincade saw to the decent burial of both Jesse Keller and Wil Logan. Both of his brothers.

As the two coffins were covered in earth, Kincade felt the medicine bag over his heart. He now understood its secrets so well. The Circle of Life—opposites—balances. He and Wil were as different as black and white. One had been raised by a caring old Indian who had found the son he had always wanted. The other was raised by a bitter mother who had wanted what the Indian had taken. Whiskey Pete had been a loyal pard to Kincade; the segundos were faithful only to their greed and lust for violence. Jesse had been full of love; Wil was full of hate. All were balanced. These balances made Kincade the man he had become.

As Kincade left Boot Hill to the tumbleweeds, he finally understood the depth and power of the beaded Circle of Life symbol on the old Indian's medicine bag.

With Wyatt's help, Kincade wired Jethro Wilcox back in Colorado that Melissa was safe. As soon as arrangements could be made, Jethro's little girl would be heading home.

The next day's telegrammed reply carried yet another surprise: "Thank God Stop Inform me date and time Stop Will meet with happy heart Stop Bringing Melissa's new mama Cissy Dye Wilcox Stop."

Kincade remembered the Dry Head Canyon. He smiled, knowing this brave woman would be the perfect one to help Melissa overcome her trauma. Cissy would do more than find her little girl's grave. She had found her chance to love little Melissa for the rest of her life.

Trains to Tombstone arrived once every week. As Kincade took care of Melissa's travel arrangements, Josephine filled her days showering love over the little girl, never leaving her side. She bathed Melissa in perfumed bubble bath. She washed her hair and tied it with ribbons. She immediately put three seamstresses to work on complete outfits—dresses, coats, satin-laced bloomers, and warm nighties. She bought Melissa shoes, stockings, and even a porcelain doll.

Melissa sat wide-eyed and silent. Her world was topsy-turvy. After being denied everything by the outlaws except one blanket, bread and water . . . after being tied by Everson in a gunnysack and lashed onto his saddle for days on end . . . she could hardly believe that this beautiful, tender, generous lady was giving her all this attention.

Josephine had a little bed put in her own room. When the nightmares came, and Melissa cried out, she would be lifted into the big featherbed and held in Josephine's safe arms until she slept again.

The train's departure day arrived. After placing the little girl's carpet satchels on board, Kincade and Josephine helped Melissa up the passenger car's steps and into the kind hands of an elderly lady who was also traveling to Colorado.

Both knew Melissa Wilcox was on her way to becoming the confident little girl she once was, when, upon reaching the train platform, she flashed them one of her dazzling smiles. "You will come visit me, please, and meet my new mama? Maybe I'll be seven by then."

Kincade and Josephine stood and waved from the station as Melissa blew kisses from the car's open window, staying there until after the train disappeared from sight. Her arm in his, the two left the platform and walked down Allen Street to the Cosmopolitan. Wyatt Earp and Doc Holliday were there, waiting for them.

"The best of mornings to you, my dear Josephine," smiled Doc, tipping his hat and bowing deeply. "You took ravishing, as usual."

"Thank you, Doc," she said. "You are, and have always been, a gentleman."

"There are a few folks who might take exception to that statement," Wyatt said.

"Brutes and louts, each and every one," replied Holliday.

Josephine turned to Kincade. "I've waited to ask you until Melissa was safely on her way. Goodness knows she's had enough of it all. But how did Wil know you were his brother? Even you didn't know."

"It struck me several days after Jess died . . ." Kincade paused, took a breath, and continued. ". . . after what Jess said in your saloon. It must have happened when the old Indian brought me into town. It was real hot that day. I took off my shirt. Wil saw the 'K' on my arm, just like the 'W' on his. He knew I was the brother he hated. He spent the rest of his life doing just that: hating me."

Josephine took Kincade's arm in hers and drew closer.

"Kincade," Wyatt said in a very official manner as Doc smiled in anticipation, coughing and smiling again. "Mr. Holliday has asked me to give something to you. Every time he saw it in the Tombstone post office, he'd laugh himself silly."

Holliday shrugged, because Wyatt's story was true. The good doctor really did think it was funny.

Marshal Wyatt Earp carefully removed something from behind his saddle, and unrolled a tattered poster, issued by and the property of the Wells Fargo Stage Line Company. At the top, one word stood out: ROBBERY! Below, and to the right, were the words: KINCADE WANTED DEAD OR ALIVE! And to the left of that was a grainy photograph of Kincade.

"Robbing a stagecoach!" said Doc Holliday with mischief in his eyes. "And here Josephine insists you are such a kind and sensitive man."

The four of them laughed heartily. "You know, Kincade," added Holliday as he looked thoughtfully at the wanted poster, "I really think that's your best side. Funny, you look much taller in the photograph than you do in person."

Another burst of laughter, which sent Doc into a fit of

coughing that would have made it all even funnier, had it not been for Holliday's deteriorating health.

"Kincade," said Wyatt, "the good doctor and I are leaving Tombstone today for a little trip up north. Word has it that the healing waters of a western Colorado town called Glenwood Springs may be just what Doc needs to cure that cough of his."

Doc raised his eyebrows, unsure of what any ground water could possibly do for him when good whiskey was all the liquid he needed. But, this Glenwood Springs would have fresh cards, players, and poker games aplenty. And that did seem like good medicine.

"I have a little favor to ask of you, Kincade," said Wyatt. Looking at Doc Holliday with a wink, Wyatt continued. "Present company excepted, of course, there's a lot of tough rabble here in Tombstone that need their attitudes adjusted upon occasion. I'll be unavailable for the task. I've seen your skills at rabble-rousing, so I would like you to sit in for me while I'm away. Raise your right hand. Without your gun, please . . ."

Kincade smiled. "Are you sure you're comfortable doing this, Wyatt? I have no experience at your job."

"Ah, but you come with excellent references," Wyatt replied, looking over to a blushing Josephine who was obviously and hopelessly in love with Kincade.

"Oh, to hell with the oath," Wyatt said as he unpinned his marshal's badge, placing it in Kincade's hand. "I've already informed Mayor Clum of your appointment, and Doc here is in a hurry. You never want to keep him waiting. It makes him grumpy. Just ask a number of the permanent residents of Boot Hill."

Wyatt reached out his hand and firmly shook Kincade's. Doc coughed into a white linen kerchief, tipping his hat to Josephine. "You will take care of our sweet Josephine, won't you, Mr. Kincade?" Doc asked as he looked toward Josie, who dazzled the three men in her black velvet prairie skirt and fitted red brocade top. Her long blond hair spilled to her waist, seductively hiding a black ribbon round her neck secured with an ivory brooch.

"Oh . . . and Kincade," Wyatt said as he and Doc Holliday stepped up and into their saddles. "That battery of guns and bullets you insist on carrying around simply won't suit your new job. I've visited with Josie, and she and I have picked out a handsome new wardrobe that befits the new marshal of Tombstone. I'm sure you'll like it."

"Extremely handsome," laughed Doc Holliday, pointing his finger at Wyatt. "You'll look just like him." And with that, Wyatt Earp and Doc Holliday rode out of the dusty town of Tombstone, Arizona Territory.

"Kincade . . . I . . ." Josephine fell silent.

Kincade stepped forward, his hands drawing Josie close into his body. His arms encircled her petite waist as she looked up into Kincade's deep blue eyes.

He spoke. "The old Indian's medicine bag tells us that for everything, there is an opposite that brings balance and meaning to life." He took his right hand and gently brushed a blond curl from Josephine's brow. She moved her hands to tenderly caress Kincade's face, her fingers running into his hair.

"And what do you suppose that means for us?" Josephine whispered as her hands moved across his chest.

Kincade paused, realizing the answer could be the most important one of his life. He drew his hands up and into hers, their fingers gently weaving four hands into two.

"Josie . . . I . . ." And he stopped. For nothing else needed to be said as their two hearts became one. Only their eyes spoke as lips tenderly met.

For all the answers, to all the questions, are always found, in the eyes.